SPORTING HITCHES

Mary B. Lyons

WORDPOWER™

SPORTING HITCHES

Copyright © Mary B. Lyons BSc(Hons) 2012

First Edition 2012
Firstclassy Fiction Series

Published in England, Great Britain, by Wordpower™
P.O. Box 1190, SANDHURST, GU47 7BW
www.wordpower.u-net.com

A CIP catalogue record for this book
Is available from the British Library

ISBN 978-0950821252

Cover and illustrations by Mary B. Lyons BSc(Hons)

Typeset by Wordpower™

Printed and bound in Great Britain by
WITLEY PRESS

About the Author

Mary B. Lyons, an established writer in several genres, was born in Surrey, England, and has been writing since the age of eight years. Those who know her will agree that she pours boundless energy, innovative creativity, positive thinking and attention to detail into any project that she undertakes. SPORTING HITCHES, a collection of short stories with illustrations, follows the publication in 2010 of her highly successful first novel, AIRSHOW ILEX and her first short story and cartoon collection, CARAVAN HITCHES in 2011. SPORTING HITCHES is the second short story collection to pour from the fingers of this talented writer and artist who deserves every success.

Writing and publishing my first novel, AIRSHOW ILEX, in 2010 was a huge undertaking. 2011 was a very busy year with many High Street book store signings, radio interviews, presenting talks to organisations and libraries as well as hosting a writing workshop at Surrey Heath Literary Festival. I also staged a photographic exhibition, featuring some of my original Farnborough International Airshow photographs, in a Hampshire library in the summer. Writing and illustrating CARAVAN HITCHES was great fun too. The launch took place in October 2011 at my solo art and photographic exhibition in Farnborough which was kindly opened by the Mayor or Rushmoor, Cr. Alex Crawford, J.P.

My next novel, CRIMSON DEEPS, will be out later this year along with a new version of my satirical, illustrated poetry book, POETRY FOR PREGNANCY which I originally published under another name some time ago.

I continue to enjoy writing and performing my songs, accompanying myself on the guitar, for various charities.

Sincere thanks to my terrific husband, Pitt, for his proof reading, critique and wonderful support.

Mary B. Lyons
Hampshire, England, 2012

Chapter		Page
1	Row, Row, Row your Boat.	1
2	Mysterious Ways.	9
3	The Deep End	20
4	Breaking the Ice.	24
5	The Amazon Marathon.	32
6	Jump to it!	41
7	Team Spirit.	45
8	In the Swim.	50
9	Sanchez.	56
10	Lucky for Some.	63
11	Ribbons.	72
12	Marooned.	75
	Pushing the Boat Out.	88
	Some farewell cartoon fun.	90

For William and Cassandra

Row, Row, Row your Boat.

'Pull! Pull! Pull!' yelled Coxy through his megaphone as the elderly rowers gave their all, emerging from under the huge stone bridge that straddled the Thames at Slivingthorne Butts on the warm, summer morning. Panting, they shipped their oars and drifted slightly sideways as the current took the Glorious Eight's boat backwards.

'It's just not good enough,' he screamed at the hunched and heaving bodies, heads down, lungs torn and panting.

'Aw, Coxy,' complained a wheezing Number Five who, at eight-two, was the oldest of the Masters' team. 'The current's strong today.'

'And it could be just the same next week when you face the Gremlin Men at the regatta.'

A seagull swooped overhead, squawking, mocking them. Charlie, a lively Number Five, pointed upwards. 'Storms at sea. Unusual in June.' He always spoke in telegrams, a leftover from his time with the post office.

'That's totally irrelevant,' continued Coxy through the megaphone. 'You lot had better get your act together or we're going to look like a load of idiots when we trail in ten lengths behind.'

Nigel, Number Four, leaned forward and tapped his mate Charlie on the shoulder. 'Pint and a pie in a minute?'

'Yes.'

'And,' continued Coxy at full volume, 'the pub is out of bounds.'

Shoulders slumped.

Two young mums pushing their prams along the towpath were smiling broadly as the instructions echoed along the riverbank. The loud groans of the eight geriatrics reached them too. One girl cupped her hands and called across to the rowers, 'Where are your walking frames then?'

'Cheek!' said Charlie, shaking his fist at them and rocking the boat.

'Furthermore,' laboured Coxy, 'there will be training in the gym every morning until the regatta.'

'What about my paper round?' Nigel enquired politely.

'Get your wife to do it.'

'Oh I couldn't possible ask her.'

The rest of the team started muttering about morning commitments... walking the dog, doctor's appointments and that sort of thing.

'Oh, alright,' boomed Coxy. 'Afternoons in the gym then, starting two o'clock tomorrow. Now, pull over to the bank.' His voice echoed like the stentorian tones of doom because they had drifted under the slime-caked arch of the bridge again.

In the boat, the team was young. Years of rowing had built up their upper body muscles and strengthened their calves and thighs. However, once out of the water, things got a bit staggery. It wasn't that they lacked strength but was more to do with balance and hip replacements.

'Lift!' They lifted.

'Over!' They turned the boat over and water poured everywhere.

'March!' Eight pairs of sinewy legs in rather wet nylon shorts, shambled and ambled to the boathouse.

The Masters had been together for donkeys' years, first at school as juveniles, collecting cups by the box-full, and then up through the rowing hierarchy to their current esteemed position as Masters' Champions three years running. Well, to be truthful, the opposition was not great. There were a couple of old boys' teams from the other side of town but the real threat was from the Gremlin Men, a group of ex-airforce types who had seen action in World War II and were, without exception, all in their eighties. They worked out of the boathouse further along but weren't there this morning.

However, a Ladies' Six shared boat storage with the elderly Glorious Eight and it was they who made the old boys straighten their backs and throw out their chests as the middle-aged women rowers took to the Thames.

'Lovely,' Charlie muttered lasciviously.

'Watch your blood pressure, old man,' Nigel said, making for the showers.

As the pub was out of bounds, the team rejoined to the cafe on the corner. Coxy came along too to keep an eye on them.

'No buns.'

'Aw, Coxy...'

'No crisps.'

'Give us a break...'

'Nine teas please, Miss, and please remove the sugar from this table.'

The girl gave him a look askance and the team shrugged as one before assuming countenances of utter dejection. In the minds of most must have been the thought that maybe it was time to pack it in and enjoy their remaining years eating toast in front of the telly.

The next afternoon in the gym, the team lined up.

'Now then, gentlemen,' Coxy said with a glint of steel in his grey eyes. 'I need some passion from you.'

'Not without my tablets,' Charlie muttered and drew sniggers as the comment was passed along the row like a Chinese whisper.

'OK. Let's get warmed up. Space out into two rows. Feet apart. That's right. Deep breath. Relax and now stretch those arms upwards.' They did as they were told. After all, Coxy had trained them to success after success for years. 'And... touch those toes.' There were a few clicking noises but they all managed it. 'And... stretch upwards again.' So it went on until it was time to take turns on the three rowing machines. While some rowed, the others pottered about doing weight lifting, stomach crunches and pull-ups.

'You were shipping far too much water today,' Coxy moaned. 'Sloppy, that's what you are.'

A bit of general disgruntled complaining went on and drew glances of disdain from some of the other gym users. What were these old codgers doing in here with their string vests, baggy shorts and hanging, wrinkled skin?

'We are the Glorious Eight and don't you forget it,' Coxy said to the rowers on the machines. 'Now, come on! Slide! Slide! Slide! Keep those shins vertical! You should be burning six hundred calories an hour instead of looking like limp rags.'

*

Nigel opened the front door. 'I'm home.'

'Dinner's nearly ready.'

There was no tempting aroma of roast beef or a Mexican casserole.

'What are we having?' he called out, as he kicked off his trainers and put his anorak in the cupboard under the stairs. He was ravenous and strolled through to the kitchen.

'Surprise!'

'What is it?'

'Sesame salad with poached cod. Just serving it up now. Come on. You must be starving.'

Nigel took his seat at the table, looked down at the repast before him and poked reluctantly at the cucumber slices.

'Oh, I had a call from Coxy this morning,' his wife said, heaping lettuce onto her plate. He looked up with interest.

'He wants you all to lose four pounds in weight before the regatta next week.'

'He rang you?'

'Oh yes. He rang all the wives and sisters. He said you can only succeed with our full support.'

'So it's rabbit food then.'

'Not entirely. You're to have pasta at teatime and a small steak for breakfast.'

'Some consolation.'

'And you've got to run for twenty minutes each day to build up your stamina.'

He groaned and surveyed the salad with desperation. The cod lay there on the plate, flaccid and congealed. She had never been good at cooking fish. He silently resolved to pack in the rowing after next week's regatta. Enough was enough.

*

'Been on at your sister as well, has he?' Nigel panted as he caught up with bachelor Charlie who was dragging himself up the slight slope that completed the first round of the block of retirement bungalows where they both lived.

'Too old,' Charlie said huskily.

'We should... take up something gentler... something involving doing not much...' Nigel said.

'What?'

'Scrabble? Chess? Cards?'

'Might.'

'Coxy will... be... dis... appointed.' (Pant, pant.)

'Yes.'

'So... will... the... womenfolk...' (Wheeze, wheeze.)

'Yes.'

'It gets us... out... of the... house...'

'Per... ma... nent... ly... at this... rate.'

They both stopped jogging and clung to a nearby gate to watch as a big, black limousine made its way slowly up the road. Their gaze followed its sedate progress until it parked a few doors up. It was a hearse.

'If that's not a... sign and a warning, I don't know... what is,' Nigel said pointedly, struggling for air.

'Agreed,' Charlie nodded sagely.

'We'll tell him... after the race.'

*

The day of the regatta had dawned fair with a strong breeze from the west. It had blown quite a gale in the night. The Glorious Eight waited to get onto the water again for the final between themselves and the Gremlin Men. Flags fluttered, stewards' boats bobbed about, the mayor was still ensconced in his stand and the banks were lined with expectant locals, cameras primed and at the ready. There was an air of jubilant expectation and amusement. This was a real scream, to see all these old codgers with their stringy arms and bald heads beavering away each year.

The Gremlin Men, with their trademark moustaches and blue caps were already in their boat. Their blades, decorated with blue gremlins, were poised and ready. The Glorious Eight got into their craft, fixed their feet in, had a couple of slides to make sure the wheels were working, and then struck out for the starting line. The Gremlin Men followed.

The starting pistol cracked and the flag went down. They were off! The Gremlins took an early lead, veering over so that as much of their wash as possible fouled their opponents' progress. Without his megaphone, Coxy resorted to hand signals, frantically gesticulating that they were to pull over further. This meant that they had even more distance to make up.

'Pull!' he mimed with his free hand. The wind was in his face and carried his voice away.

The Gremlin Men grinned through their moustaches as they took a two-length lead immediately ahead of the champions. The curve in the river was coming up. The current was strong as it passed the island.

'Going right,' yelled the Gremlins' cox, putting his arm out. He wanted to take full advantage of the current. Behind them, the Glorious Eight struggled on, dentures clenched, striped blades dipping in and out, in and out, working as one machine but it was hopeless. They had just passed under the footbridge that joined the bank to the island, when they heard shouting and glanced back up.

A row of women wearing sunglasses were waving and screaming to them.

'Yoo-hoo! Yoo-hoo!' Then one shouted, 'Now!' and they lifted the fronts of their tee-shirts, baring their all to eight elderly rowers who nearly let their oars fall out of the rowlocks in surprise. The Gremlin Men, with their peaked caps and heads down, had missed the show but the impetus was enough to give the Glorious Eight the push they needed.

In and out, in and out, in and out, went the oars as the men worked like demons. The Gremlins, so sure of victory, turned their heads slowly in amazement, as eight tittivated geriatrics zoomed past, backs straight, strokes sure and Coxy grinning like a lunatic. Over the finishing line they lunged. The hooter tooted. The crowd at the finish went crazy, whistling and singing. The cup was theirs once more.

*

Coxy sat with the team in the clubhouse. Egg and cress sandwiches, home made cakes and refreshments were being hungrily devoured by everybody. The tea-urn steamed away in the corner. The wives and sisters surveyed their men-folk with innocent pride. They would, no doubt, be informed later by rumour and gossip why the team had put such a spurt on.

'Oh well done, lads!' Coxy demurred, pride all over his face. The Glorious Eight were still tickled pink at what had happened. The buzz in the clubroom was so loud that they could hardly hear themselves speak.

'Who were they?' Nigel asked. 'Where did those women come from? I looked up and, suddenly, they appeared!'

Only Coxy, with a smug smile, was in the know. It had cost him a hundred pounds but that middle-aged ladies' rowing team were jolly good sports.

'Have a sandwich,' he said to Nigel. 'Here's to next year!'

Mysterious Ways

'Father, we simply cannot have girls hanging around the pitch while the team is practising.'

Mrs. Fotherwaite-Smythe sat in the vestry of St. Bolod's Church, bristling with puritanical rage.

'It's rather difficult, you see,' the priest said. 'Some of the boys are at that age. Don't forget, I take confessions.' He touched the side of his nose with a knowing wink.

'Well I am going to write to the bishop about it. The church football pitch was installed to keep male teenagers out of mischief, not encourage them into it.'

Father Nicholas put the tips of his fingers together and peered at her over his half-glasses.

'My dear lady, all those girls out there,' - he indicated through the window -, 'are handmaidens of the church. They do the flowers, as you know, sing in the choir and help with the brownies. If we upset them, it would be really most inconvenient.'

'Poppycock!' She stood up, wobbling with anger. 'When I was a girl (she pronounced it to rhyme with 'bell') we would never have been allowed near such moral danger!'

She flounced from the sacristy, genuflected humbly as she passed the central aisle, and then made here way out of the side door of the church.

Father Nicholas rose as she left, shook his head, pushed his chair away and went over to look out of the latticed window. Why did teenage girls have to scream so loudly? The boys' team, playing six-a-side, including their spare, were panting up and down the pitch, dribbling, dodging, shooting goals and leaping about with delight when somebody scored. This incited the girls to dizzy heights of vertical take-off, clapping and hugging each other. He smiled knowingly. Ah, to be young again! People always thought priests had no history of romance, but he could have told a tale or two of summer camps and dusky, warm evenings, long grass and the scent of a girl's flowing hair.

The volunteer trainer blew his whistle and the practice came to a stop as the sweating boys gathered around him.

'Well done, lads! Well done!' He slapped a couple of them on the shoulders in congratulatory fashion. 'You'll wipe the floor with that team from the Mossington Estate Community Centre next Saturday. Now then, can you all spare an hour on Friday evening for a spot of training?' The team muttered and agreed that they could. 'I'm proud of you. Real proud of you.' He smiled encouragingly. 'Now, off to the changing rooms, lock up and bring me the key. Hey, don't forget to put the ball away!' He pointed at it and then went to gather up the tray with chewed orange peel on it.

'Sir,' said one of the girls, Monica, sidling over. 'Can we play soccer too?' The others giggled.

'What did you say?'

'Can we play too?'

He stood up, fingers sticky with juice from the tray, and surveyed the bunch of teenage girls before him. Without exception, they were plastered in heavy make-up, their hair was coiffured into extraordinary concoctions that brought to mind words like 'hurricane' and 'hedge backwards' and they wore inordinately short skirts.

'You want to play football? But you're girls. It's a boy's game.'

'Begging your pardon, sir, but there are lots of ladies soccer teams now.'

'That's as maybe but not here at St. Bolod's. Who would train you anyway? You need a lady trainer.'

'Oh, we're not fussy,' one said. 'You can train us. Look how fit we are.' With that, they all started running on the spot and then launched into star jumps, hair flopping all over the place. The November Saturday afternoon was drawing in. Mist hung over the edge of the field and it would be another frosty night. Their breath emerged in white puffs.'

'Alright,' he said with an exhausted sigh, 'let me think about it. How many of you want to play?'

'All of us.'

He counted seven. 'That's not a team,' he said.

'It is for six-a-side.' They were not going to be put down.

'Leave it with me.'

The boys, swigging from bottles of water, started to filter out of the changing room. One came over and gave the key to the trainer. The girls hastily tidied their dishevelled hair, stuck out their chests and minced towards the boys.

'Run!' yelled the goalie and they did.

'Spoilsports! We'll get you!' shouted the girls' leader.

'Nah nah nee nah-nah!' called the boys, taunting, as they jogged out through the gates.

The trainer thought it was all a bit loud.

'Come along now, ladies. Quieten down a bit. We don't want the neighbours complaining.' He nodded towards the row of suburban semi-detacheds that backed onto the pitch.

'Are you coming to the match next Saturday?'

'You bet, sir.'

'I'll probably be able to tell you then if you can play or not. There's a church committee meeting on Thursday night. I'll drop a note to the secretary for you but I don't hold out high hopes. Now, off you go. You shouldn't be hanging around. It's getting cold.' As they walked away, he marvelled at the brave show of legs on such a nippy afternoon. He tipped the orange peel and tray into a plastic carrier bag, wiped his fingers on a tissue and strolled over to his car.

*

Mrs. Fotherwaite-Smythe knelt in the confessional. 'Bless me Father for I have sinned. It is one week since my last confession and these are my sins.'

Through the mesh grill, Father Nicholas could smell the booze on her breath. He knew who it was. He sat there, hand to one temple, listening intently to the petty sins of a sad and lonely widow.

'I was vain, this week, Father. I kept looking at my reflection in shop windows. I was jealous of my neighbour's new car and, worst of all, I pretended to be out when a charity collector came.'

The priest uttered a few words of advice about how to avoid these sins in the future, asked her to say a prayer of contrition and go forth with a firm purpose of amendment. He gave her a penance of five 'Our Fathers'. 'Go in peace and may God bless you. Pray for me.'

'Yes, Father.' The confessional door creaked as the elderly lady rose and opened it, leaving imprints of her very chubby knees indented in the red velvet kneeler and the aroma of her whisky lingering in the air. The priest always pretended that he didn't know who it was. Through a crack he could see a few more customers lined up to unburden themselves. He steeled himself as the next one came in sniffing loudly and suspiciously before kneeling down to make her confession.

*

At the very end of the regular Thursday night committee meeting, the chairman enquired, 'Any other business?' Rain plopped depressingly into a bucket in the corner as the damp stain on the ceiling spread and the winter wind whistled through the ill-fitting window. The members were keen to get home to their cosy central heating.

The secretary, muffled up in a woollen coat and hat, unfolded a piece of paper. 'We've had a request from the youth football team trainer to allow girls to form a team and be trained here on our pitch.'

'Girls?' (to rhyme with bells). 'Football? Here at St. Bolod's?' The question bore all the timbre of Oscar Wilde's 'A handbag?'

'Yes,' said the secretary. 'Girls.'

'Well,' bristled Mrs. Fotherwaite-Smythe, black spotted hat veil wobbling above her real fur coat, 'I've never heard of such a thing. It is bad enough that they stand around cheering and flaunting themselves...'

'One moment please, my dear,' said Father Nicholas affably, seeking to defuse the protestation. 'These would be our handmaidens again, would it?'

'Yes,' said the secretary, 'the stalwart group that is the backbone of the choir and helps Brown Owl with the brownies. My granddaughter had just got her cookery badge,' she added with pride.

Mrs. Fotherwaite-Smythe's face grew much redder. 'May I remind the committee that my late husband left a rather considerable amount of money towards the restoration of the church tower and that I myself, have decreed in my will that the rebuilding of the sacristy will be funded from my estate, when I pass to a better place.' She lowered her head thoughtfully at the possibility of her own demise. The priest lowered his too and wondered how much longer the sacristy roof would hold out and which would go first. 'We'd better put it to the vote,' he said.

'That's not all,' the florid widow added. 'I also suggest that girls should not be allowed on the church football field when the boys are practising.'

'Please raise your hands if you agree,' said the chairman. Silence and hesitant looks.

The committee was church mouse poor in liquid funds for restoration work. They all put their hands up.

'Carried unanimously,' said the chairman, packing his briefcase. The meeting was over.

*

'Sir, sir, said the girls' leader,' catching up with the trainer by the turnstile.

He looked down at her sympathetically. 'I'm really sorry,' he said, 'but the committee voted against girls playing football on church land.'

'That is so rotten unfair!' she protested. 'Who voted against it? Tell me!'

'I'm afraid they all did.'

'Why? We'll be as good as the boys are.' Her friends came over, drawn by her waving arms and angry face. 'They won't have us.'

'What?' the others jabbered away angrily.

'Well, we'll see about that,' she said mysteriously. 'Come on.' They all left in a huddle.

'I'm really sorry...' said the trainer to thin air.

*

A fortnight later, on a Sunday afternoon, the bishop came to give his annual homily. It was visit eagerly anticipated with pleasure by Father Nicholas who was in the presbytery, taking tea with the right reverend the Lord Bishop. When the telephone rang in the hall, the housekeeper wiped her hands on her floral pinafore and walked through to lift the receiver.

'I'm afraid he's with the bishop,' she said in a whisper behind a cupped hand.

'Tell Father it's urgent. I must speak to him.'

'Very well, but it's most impolite to disturb the Bishop. Hold on a moment please.'

She knocked gently and went into the dark panelled dining room and coughed discreetly. The priest turned and looked enquiringly at her. She walked softly over to him and whispered in his ear.

'Forgive me, your reverend, but I must take an urgent call. I shouldn't be long. Please, have another slice of cake.'

Father Nicholas hurried into the hall and lifted the receiver. It was the church committee secretary and she was frantic.

'What? No flowers? No choir?' he said in utter dismay. He looked at his watch. People galore would be arriving for the ceremony in an hour. 'What shall we do?'

'The shops are shut and it's too far to go to the out of town supermarket and back. I'll pick some chrysanths from the garden. I should be with you in half an hour.'

'What about the singing? We must have singing.'

'I can't help you there... hold on... I've got a CD that might do. Must dash.' She was gone.

As he went to go back into the dining room, the 'phone rang again. This time it was the sacristan who trained and organised the altar boys.

'On strike?' the priest said with alarm.

'Yes. They say some of their brothers are in the football team and some of their sisters are handmaidens. Something to do with girls and football?'

'I knew this would end in tears,' said the priest aloud in a whisper. He dialled Mrs. Fotherwaite-Smythe. She sounded as if she was three sheets to the wind. Sunday afternoon was a lonely time for a widow. He explained the situation to her. She seemed to be having trouble understanding.

'Are you alright?' he asked. The line went dead. He dashed back to the dining room, apologised, urged the Bishop to eat yet more cake, told the housekeeper to make another pot of tea, then rushed out to his car. He was about to drive to the unhappy widow's huge house in Magnolia Drive. However, as he came along next to his church, he saw a band of teenagers with banners proclaiming, 'Football for all', 'Sex Equality in the Church' and 'Equal rights for lady footballers'. He pulled up beside them. There were all the handmaidens, the boys' football team, the altar boys and some others he didn't really know.

'What is going on?' he demanded.

'We're on strike,' they chanted in unison. 'Strike! Strike! Strike for equality!'

Leaving the engine running, he got out and waved at them before slamming both his hands on the bonnet. The silence was instant. 'I've got an emergency. Who knows first aid?' Three of the girls put their hands up.

'Come with me. Get in. Any of you got a mobile 'phone? Yes? Call an ambulance and send it to *The Ridings* in Magnolia Avenue. I think one of our committee members is ill.' He put the car into gear. 'Do up your seat-belts.' He broke the speed limit. Time to confess that later. The car screeched to a halt outside Mrs. Fotherwaite-Smythe's grand house. The gates were closed. They all got out and rushed up to the front door, ringing the bell and hammering loudly. There was no response.

Father Nicholas trod on a flowerbed and peered in through the lounge window. His parishioner was on the floor. Her arm was covered in blood. Her eyes were closed. The girls crowded around him. Where was that ambulance?

'Shall I go round the back, Father, and see if I can get in there?'

'Yes, yes. Please do.' He hammered on the window. 'Mrs. Fotherwaite-Smythe! Wake up! It's me, Father Nicholas.' She didn't move. Then he heard the tinkle of glass breaking and a minute later two of the girls were leaning over the patient in the lounge while the third opened the front door to let the priest in.

'She's bleeding heavily,' said Monica. 'Here, wrap my scarf tightly around her elbow, apply pressure and hold her arm up. She cut it on that glass when she fell. Mind you don't kneel on it.' Then she pushed the old lady onto her side and covered her with her anorak and a rug from the sofa.

'Do you know what you're doing?' the priest asked anxiously.

'She does,' said one of the others. 'We all do. We went on a course.'

Suddenly, Mrs. Fotherwaite-Smythe uttered a spluttering sort of cough, followed by a deep breath. Her eyes flew open as she lay there on the washed Persian carpet, which it has to be said, was rather awash with its owner's blood.

'What are you doing in my house?' she demanded.

'Saving your life, by the look of it,' said the priest.

The sound of the ambulance siren grew nearer.

'Quickly, go and let them in!'

*

'I want to thank you young people most sincerely,' said Mrs. Fotherwaite-Smythe in her hospital bed a few days later. Monica and her two friends stood looking and feeling rather embarrassed.

'Father Nicholas told me what you did. You saved my life. Thank you.'

'That's alright,' said Monica. 'It was rather exciting.'

'Maybe but I want to show my overwhelming gratitude to you all.'

'Oh, there's no need...'

'But there is.' She raised her good arm. A nurse came over.

'Now, we mustn't tire you out, must we? You've had a nasty accident. I'm guessing that you three are the ones who came to this lady's rescue.'

'Well, it was really Monica...'

The trio felt very awkward.

'We all did it,' Monica said. The nurse smiled and moved on to attend to the next patient. Father Nicholas appeared.

'Hello. I'm glad you got my message to come and visit. Have you heard the good news yet?' They shook their heads. He took the old lady's hand in his. 'Mrs. Fotherwaite-Smythe has graciously offered to sponsor a girls' football team at St. Bolod's.' The three giggled and smiled. 'This includes buying your strip and paying for your transport to matches.'

'Wow!'

'And the boys' trainer will train you and enter you into a girls' six-a-side league. How does that sound?'

'Brilliant,' they all agreed.

'In the spirit of forgiveness, I shall draw a veil over the disastrous visit by the Bishop. When he comes to take the confirmation service next month, I hope,' and he paused knowingly, 'that we shall again have our full complement of handmaidens and altar boys.'

'Oh, yes, Father. You will.'

'Good. There's one more thing...'

'Yes?'

'We've decided to call your team 'The Fotherwaites.' The girls agreed that in the circumstances, it was a good name. They thanked their benefactress and left, very happy.

'Well, I'd better be off too,' said the priest.

'Just a moment. I've got something here for you,' said the patient. 'Please take it.'

*

Outside in the gathering dusk, Father Nicholas opened the envelope. A cheque for £200,000 pounds. More than enough to rebuild the sacristy. He smiled and shook his head in disbelief.

'Well, you do work in mysterious ways,' he whispered, tucking It carefully in his black cassock pocket as he dodged the puddles in the hospital car park.

The Deep End

Ellie sat dangling her feet in the warm blue water. The smell of chlorine was strong. She looked down at her new red swimsuit. It made the best of her full figure. In the deep end, Marcus was treading water and flirting with the other advanced class swimmers. She could see his white teeth shining against his sun-tanned face as he threw back his head laughing.

'Ready to take the plunge?' enquired Jak, the tall, fair Scandinavian instructor. There was kindness in his voice.

'Yes,' she replied. 'It feels warmer than last week.'

Grasping the side of the steps, she eased herself into the pool and ducked down so that her shoulders were under water. It was like this every time. Marcus plunged in and swam like a happy dolphin, grinning, ploughing along the lanes, his blue-tinted goggles catching the lights, his broad shoulders displaying body-builder muscles.

In the shallow end, Ellie held onto the bar and thrashed about on her front as her chubby legs beat the surface behind her, churning it up so that the lane slaves had to make little detours as they passed. She let go and took her feet off the bottom, making breast-strokes with her arms but always keeping her toes just inches from the floor of the pool. She didn't really swim.

Jak paraded back and forth as instructors do. There was a lifeguard on duty too but he was now chatting avidly with the advanced swimmers in the deep end, joining in the banter and fun generated by Marcus. It was the same where-ever they went. Ellie lay on her back, holding on to the bar, and let her legs float to the surface, gently paddling.

'When are you going to start swimming again?' asked Jak, crouching down on the wet tiles to chat. She looked at him, upside down, then turned over and stood, waist-high in the shallow end.

'I can see you have swum before,' he said. 'Why don't you do it now?'

She smiled at his charming accent. 'I lost my nerve.'

'Would you like a board?'

'Aren't they only for children?'

He walked over to the rack on the wall and took a bashed about polystyrene oblong and handed it down to her. 'Have a go with that,' he said. 'It'll give you confidence.'

Feeling rather foolish, she accepted the pitted object and held onto it with both hands, floating about a little as he gave her an encouraging smile before going over to talk to some others who were speed training in the far three lanes.

A wave washed over her, knocking her off balance, so that she stood up suddenly and angrily. 'Why did you do that...?' she started to ask and then realised it was Marcus larking about, greatly amused.

'Why don't you swim with me?' he asked, touching her arm and pulling at it gently. 'Come on! You'll love it in the four metres. The water holds you up.'

She grabbed the side, carelessly letting the little white board float away.

'No. No thank you. I'm fine here. You go and do your lengths.'

He smacked the surface playfully with his hand and then turned and disappeared beneath it like a submarine, only to emerge further along, creating a bow wave that charted his progress down the lane.

So the session passed, with Marcus clocking up length after length while Ellie dabbled in the shallow end, enduring the pitying glances of the real swimmers.

Afterwards in the changing room she stood dripping, feet feeling squidgey on the concrete floor, trying to cover herself with a towel that always seemed inadequate. How the people in her company would laugh if they could see how pathetic she appeared in the water... she the managing director of one of the largest export businesses in the country!

'How many lengths tonight?' she asked Marcus as they walked through reception on their way to the car.

'Oh, only thirty. I spent too much time chatting down the deep end!' He draped his arm across her shoulders. 'Now when are you going to join me there? Eh?' He pushed open the swing door and they went through together.

*

It was the last session before Christmas. Jak, the tall, blond instructor, nearly overtook Ellie in the corridor on his way to the men's changing rooms. 'Good evening.'

'Hello Jak. Nice to see you again.'

'I didn't recognise you. It must be... let me see... two years since you were last here. I wondered what happened to you both. Suddenly you didn't come any more... but you are looking very well.'

Ellie hesitated. 'Thank you.' She paused. 'Marcus and I aren't together now.'

'I'm sorry to hear that.'

'It's OK.' She smiled with a hint of chagrin and pushed open the door to the ladies' changing rooms.

The shower didn't feel very warm but she went under it as requested. Not many people were in the pool this evening.

'Too busy doing last minute shopping,' she thought.

When she reached the pool area Jak was already in the water. She walked along the tiled edge and climbed down the steps into the welcome warmth.

'You're in!' she said with surprise, seeing him standing waist-deep waiting for her.

'I'm off duty.'

'I hope you have a staff pass.'

'Yes, I do. Free.'

'That's nice.'

'I'm just going for a little swim. Won't you join me?'

She viewed him suspiciously.

'I know you can swim,' he said.

She adjusted her shoulder strap unnecessarily.

'You can stop pretending now,' he added.

She turned away, tears smarting in her eyes.

'Let's go!' he said, tapping her lightly on the arm, and they did... all the way to the deep end.

23

MARY B. LYONS

Breaking the Ice

Golf Club captain Fenella Wrythe-Grately threw down her pencil and put her elbows on the committee room table.

'We've got to do something memorable this year,' she said, cupping her chin in the palms of her hands. She was a small, fine-boned woman whose slender frame belied her navvy's swing. As a prematurely retired civil servant she poured the frustrations of her empty middle-aged life into this unpaid job. Next to her, TK, chairman of this, the Pitt Estate Golf Club, threw up his hands in despair.

'We've exhausted our repertoire,' he said resignedly.

'Rubbish!' retorted Fenella, thumping the Friday afternoon table defiantly. 'We're bound to come up with something.'

'Well,' interjected Jon-Jon, the grey-haired treasurer, leaning back in his chair and gazing moodily out onto the November course. 'I think this annual match against Filby Park Club is getting the teensiest bit boring.' He paused to assess the impact his words had made. 'Take last year,' he drawled, turning his head lazily towards the others, 'I know it was their turn to choose and half of their team went down with 'flu' but, frankly, their last minute announcement of Members of Parliament was pathetic,' he chortled.

'Time's getting on rather,' said TK a trifle uncomfortably, squinting at his digital gold watch and remembering with pleasure the full, curly white wig he had worn as a lord on that occasion. 'I'll give you until Monday, Fenella,' he said, 'but if we haven't come up with something suitable by then, we'll have to cancel.' He closed his folder and looked sternly over his pince-nez. 'Any other business?'

Fenella opened her mouth to speak but quickly shut it again.

'Meeting closed.'

*

24

Pitt Estate Golf Club had been established for ninety years as had its rival, the Filby Park Club. Throughout the decades, even during the wars, the rival members had duly turned out in themed fancy dress each Boxing Day in an attempt to thrash the opposition. Who actually won had become a secondary consideration. A challenging theme was the prime objective.

Fenella lay on her back in the middle of her king-size bed, gazing at the midnight ceiling as themes of previous matches drifted into her fading consciousness. Over the years every notable period of history had been depicted, as had space travel, doctors and nurses, vicars and ladies of ill repute, pantomimes, politicians, uniforms, national costumes and circuses, as well as wild animals and underwater life.

She would never forget octopus Basil grappling with his tentacles at the seventh! Oh, and what about Simon rotating on the spot with his 'Jaws' fin in a high wind? She drifted off into sleep to be visited all night by Elizabethan ladies, clowns and surgeons. By dawn she was exhausted and depressed. This was a point of honour. If they gave up now it would reflect badly upon her and she wasn't going to have that!

*

On Monday morning Fenella was waiting in the chairman's office to greet him. More than a little bleary from a jolly Sunday night spent at the nineteenth, he put his briefcase down on the leather-topped desk and eased his ample form into the reclining swivel chair.

'Good weekend?'

'Not too bad,' she lied.

'Well?'

'I've got it!' Fenella said.

*

'My ball's split!' wailed Bernard from his misty lie behind the fifth.

'I told you not to use those cheap ones in this frost,' retorted Simon, adjusting his toga with an air of superiority. 'Here, take one of my super-duper, three-layered efforts with the non-freezing liquid centre and elastic windings.'

'I would if I could see where you were,' called Bernard across the snow that coated the course in drifts from end to end.

'Over here!' called Simon. 'To you!'

There was a muffled 'zing' and the bright pink ball flew through the damp air to hit Bernard's bare ankle decidedly sharply.

'Youch!' He lifted his leg, wincing with pain.

'Playing through!' called the Filby Club's ladies' champion, sporting a white sheeting toga, tinsel coronet and purple arms. Simon stood aside and watched as she swaggered past him. As soon as she'd gone, he played over to Bernard.

'I'm not supposed to change ball type during a match, am I?' queried the hopping slave, very glad that he had altered his mind and not worn sandals.

'Who's going to know?' replied his emperor friend grinning conspiratorially. 'Why don't you rub some snow into that. It's turning blue.'

'It's not the only thing,' retorted his partner wryly.

Further down the course, Fenella and Jacqui struggled along through the drifts chained together as two slave girls.

'Whose stupid brainchild was this?' demanded the latter.

'It seemed a good idea at the time,' grimaced Fenella, wishing she'd come unshackled.

'Stand behind me and hold onto my wrist while I play this stroke.'

'Say, look at that!' Jacqui's white cloud of breath hissed into Fenella's ear.

Through the mist, across the fairway, the chairman in a mini-tunic composed skilfully of two white pillow slips pegged together and belted with green tinsel, bent over to reveal his red tartan underpants flashing contrastingly against the white landscape peopled with monochromatic figures.

'Get a move on, old chap,' cajoled Jon-Jon the treasurer, rattling the sword of his gladiator's outfit.

'Don't rush me!'

'My leather thonging's going stiff and this hardware's darned chilly against the vitals.'

The ball rolled uncertainly in a wavering arc around the cleared around hole and came to a rest defiantly on the other side of it. The chairman kicked it in with his foot.

'Cheat!' said the treasurer, adjusting his under-sized helmet.

'I meant to have a word with you about your expenses,' replied TK.

'Jolly good shot!' exclaimed the treasurer loudly, upon instant reflection.

'Thought you'd see it my way,' replied his partner smugly.

'Baah-de-baah-de-baah-baah!'

Players stopped in mid-stroke to turn and observe 'Nero' driving a two-wheeled chariot down the fairway. It was pulled by two "horses' wearing donkey heads borrowed from the local amateur dramatic society's last year's production of *A Midsummer Night's Dream*. A loud clanking could be heard from snow-chains attached to the Ben Hur style wheels. The few hardy spectators cheered. TK grabbed Jon-Jon's wrist. 'Good Heavens!' he exclaimed with whisky-heavy breath. 'It's Filby's trump card!'

'Going to ruin the flaming course!' said Jon-Jon, peering after his ball into the mist.

Filby Club had certainly cocked a snook at their hosts. 'Nero' lashed his stallions unmercifully with the multi-tailed string and tinsel whip. 'More! More!' shouted the muffled horses, pawing the ground in their spiked shoes. The trumpeter walking beside the chariot blasted on his horn continuously.

Distracted by the commotion, Jon-Jon had miss-hit his ball causing it to veer to the left towards Little Serpentine pond. He was somewhat distressed that it had landed smack in the middle of the ice.

'Oh no!' he gasped with despair.

'What'd you say, old chap?' enquired TK vaguely.

'My ball! It's on the ice!'

'Rules say you can play it,' guffawed TK. 'Come on! Let's see you try!'

Dragging their trolleys, the pair trudged through the snow to the perimeter of the frozen water. A few spiky reeds poked out at the edge. TK brought his five-iron down with a smart crack on the surface. It was rock hard.

'Looks firm enough to me,' he said confidently. 'Test it. Give me your hand!'

Gingerly, Jon-Jon placed one tentative foot on the ice and then the other. He bounced up and down a little but nothing beneath him moved.

'Hand me that wood, please,' he said cautiously to the chairman, who duly obliged. Then he set out to cover the ten yards to where his ball lay.

Simon and limping Bernard abandoned the Nero spectacular and came over to watch their team mate pad and slither carefully over the ice. All was going well until Jon-Jon was within two yards of his objective when suddenly there was a loud and distinct 'crack!' All conversation ceased. The treasurer stood there, frozen as if part of the pond, and spoke through clenched teeth.

'Did you hear that?' he said with a tremulous voice.

They all nodded. Silence. They waited.

'Baah-de-baah-de-baah!' tooted the trumpeter, now on board the horse-drawn chariot with 'Nero' as it came flying and sliding around from behind Clinton's Copse and drove onto the ice from the far side.

'NO!' shrieked the Pitt Estate team unanimously but it was too late. The momentum took the chariot across the surface to within inches of Jon-Jon, and then, like some ghastly, slow motion movie, chariot, horses, 'Nero' and one very angry gladiator descended on a fragmenting platform of ice into two feet of freezing cold and rather slimy, Boxing Day water.

The shackled girls came panting up to the scene of devastation. The chariot was on its side. The papier-mâché horses' heads were deteriorating into something resembling the Elephant Man. 'Nero' thrashed about in the water angrily while his trumpeter rummaged beneath the icy surface for his instrument. Jon-Jon lay pale and slumped with only his head and arms out of the water as he clung limply to a wheel in a semi-faint. A great deal of colourful language filled the air.

'Come on!' said Fenella setting off across the ice, followed by her reluctant companion who had no choice but to go under protest. The surface soon gave way beneath them, plunging goose-pimpled legs into the icy water but, with the others, they hauled the treasurer back to the bank.

'He's stopped breathing!' declared Jacquie, bursting into tears.

'Artificial respiration! Mouth to mouth!' declared Fenella.

And that is how the treasurer opened his eyes some minutes later to find himself being passionately and alternately kissed by two shackled slave-girls who were taking turns to get him breathing again.

'I've died and gone to heaven, haven't I?' he said incredulously.

'Have a nip of this, old boy!' said TK, producing his famous hip-flask.

Icicles were forming on the togas and tunics of the frozen and bedraggled group that lifted Jon-Jon from the ground and carried him shivering and chattering into the clubhouse, thronged by the onlookers who had certainly got more entertainment than in previous years. Snow had started to fall again so the match was abandoned.

*

In the men's shower room, the perma-frosted players luxuriated beneath the warm overhead sprays in a row along the wall. Jon-Jon had gone off to Casualty for a check-up, somebody had found the key to the girls' padlock and they were all looking forward to their Boxing Day dinner. The Chairman started to sing the unofficial club song.

'We're the members of the Pitt's Estate Golf Club,

We like to hit our balls, not linger in the pub.'

The others joined in.

'Driving down the fairway, scrabbling in the rough,

Always stuck in bunkers. We never get enough!'

Then it got a lot bawdier.

In the steam of the ladies' shower room next door, Jacqui passed the soap over the cubicle wall to Fenella and said, 'Just listen to the boys! They've had a morning to remember!'

'Mmm,' said Fenella, scrubbing away to restore her circulation. 'So have we. I thought I'd never be warm again.'

'Are you going to stay for the meal?' asked Jacqui, emptying the last of the shampoo over her short, dark hair.

'Yes,' replied her friend, 'but then I'm off to the hospital to see Jon-Jon.'

'I didn't know you two were close,' replied Jacquie incredulously, sticking her head around the plastic curtain.

'What a kisser!' said Fenella with a sigh.

'But he's...' started Jacquie.

'Unattached?' cut in Fenella whimsically.

'Well, I didn't think he was the...'

'Marrying kind?'

'He lives with his...'

'Mother.'

'Yes, how did you know?'

'I've been dating him for three months. Old fashioned type. He hadn't kissed me until today.'

'You're a dark horse!'

'Yes, but not into pulling chariots!' she chortled and they both laughed and laughed.

The Amazon Marathon

'There's a letter too,' the solicitor said, sliding a cream coloured envelope across his leather-topped, mahogany desk towards the shocked young man on the other side.

'I can't believe this. I was supposed to inherit everything from the old boy.'

'Go on, open it, Darnley.'

Reluctantly, the disappointed beneficiary ripped the envelope and read:

Dearest Nephew,

You have enjoyed the very best of everything throughout your spoiled life and it seems to me that it would be against all natural justice for you to inherit my vast estate when you have contributed nothing whatsoever to the universe. True, it was most unfortunate that you lost your parents when you were so young, but if you are reading this then I, your former guardian, must also have shuffled off this mortal coil. I would not be doing you any favours if I let you go further into your wasteful life without pointing you in the right direction.

Therefore, before you may claim your inheritance, I decree that you must use those running skills of yours (and let us be frank, that's the only thing you picked up at university before you flunked out) to run a marathon for charity. Furthermore, it should not be just any old marathon but a truly challenging one. So, Darnley, you will run in the Amazon Log Road Marathon. You must also be sponsored to the tune of one million pounds, the proceeds of which will be donated to saving the Brazilian Rain Forest.

With affection,

Uncle.

Darnley folded the letter and put it in his corduroy jacket pocket. He got up and leaned across the desk to shake hands with the family solicitor.

'I don't have any choice, do I?'

'No, I'm afraid you don't.'

'What happens to the inheritance if I fail to complete the task?'

'The Treasury will have a very nice windfall. It might make a dent in the national debt,' the older man joked, rising to his feet. Then he coughed with embarrassment and said, 'but I'm sure you'll do very well. Get the organisers to write to me when it's over. I'll need some proof.'

Darnley left the office with his heart pounding.

As soon as he was back in his Belgravia flat, he searched the internet for details of the specified marathon. The next one was in three months time, just before the start of the rainy season. The closing date was in a fortnight. The entry fee was two hundred pounds. He downloaded a form, filled it in, emailed it and paid the fee on his only valid credit card. Where it had asked about sponsorship, he had written 'to be advised before the closing date.' That bought him a little time.

He punched in Cedric's number.

'Yes?' said a crisp, upper crust voice.

'Cedric, old chum, it's Darnley. I need your sparkling brain. Get yourself over here immediately.'

'I say...'

'No arguments. If you want our lifestyle to continue, move yourself.' He hung up.

'You'll need a trainer and hundreds of sponsors,' Cedric extolled breathlessly half an hour later. The first part's easy but you simply have to get on television with a heart-wrenching story for the rest of it. I'll have a word with my cousin. She's a producer on *Dayways,* the daily magazine programme.'

Darnley nodded enthusiastically in agreement. 'Now, what can my sob story be about?'

'Bereaved orphan and nephew fulfils deceased guardian's last wish,' Cedric announced with conviction. 'I can see the headlines now.' He waved his finger in a circle in the air. 'Ah, yes, we can mention your health problem.'

'What? I don't have one.'

'Leave it with me. Here's the name of a really good trainer. It'll cost you but he's worth every penny. I'd better get busy. See you later.' What were a few more debts, after all?

*

'Your transponder came this morning,' said the trainer, waving a small, neat package at Darnley. 'The marathon organisers have given one to everybody in the race.'

'You mean that timer thing that I have to wear?'

'Yes, they'll be able to clock your start and finish most accurately. Actually, this is going to be quite good because although there are about twenty thousand runners and the race will be started with the gun, they will actually time you from mat to mat.'

'Mat? What mat?'

'You have to run over a special electronic detection mat at each end and it will pick up your time automatically.'

'Where does this transponder thing go?'

'On your chest. There was a choice of shoe or chest but I always feel you could get unlucky at the finish and end up with it on your back foot when it's your chest that has to pass the line.'

'Good thinking.'

Darnley burst into a spate of running on the spot.

'How are you feeling confidence-wise? You've done all this sort of thing before, haven't you?'

'Only for my university. I came in first quite a few times.'

'Well, it shouldn't be a problem. I mean, you don't have to win, just get over the finishing line. I gather from Cedric that your T.V. appearance was a stunner.'

'Er, yes.' Darnley still felt rather bad about it. While it had been one thing to talk in a choked up voice about the loss of his parents and uncle (thank goodness for those drama lessons!) it had been quite another to throw in a painful and incurable back problem. Half an onion in his handkerchief, to produce tears, had rather pushed things. The result, though, had been spectacular and sponsorship was still pouring in. He would surely hit his target of a million pounds.

*

The loudspeakers announced in Portuguese, English, German and French that it was five minutes to the starting pistol. Thousands of runners were jogging on the spot and limbering up as they waited, corralled in square pens.

'Bang!' went the gun. The first contingent hit the dusty, orange, Amazon Log Road track. Others poured out behind them and the seething mass of bobbing athletes paced themselves at the start of the 42,195 metres, thudding in the historic footsteps of Pheidippides, the Greek messenger from the Battle of Marathon.

It was a humid, overcast day. The crowds lining the start had been enthusiastic and loud, cheering and waving flags and, as the runners thinned out and a light breeze picked up, Darnley felt exhilarated and hopeful. He had trained hard. All he had to do was to finish and uncle's fortune would be his.

About twenty kilometres in, just before the half-way point, the first drops of rain started to plop onto the dusty track, exploding like miniature mines or bubbles in boiling custard. It was refreshing to begin with but soon escalated into a steady downpour that soaked the runners so that their vests stuck to their chests like wrinkled second skins. The lush Rainforest on either side looked dark and inviting for the tree canopy would surely give shelter. No. He should keep going. You never knew what was lurking in there. Anyway, a refreshment point was coming up.

'Here you are young fella-me-lad,' said the official as he handed an open bottle of spring water to Darnley as he ran past, his trainers sploshing in the orange mud. A slight slope lay ahead and the rain was coming down in sheets that made visibility difficult. Suddenly, Darnley was alarmed to see a torrent of water racing towards him. Instinct told him to get out of the way. So he diverted his steps sideways over a low bank of sticky mud, jumped the drainage channel and found himself just inside the edge of the forest, the floor of which was also swimming in water. A loud rushing noise prompted him to look around in panic for a tree to climb up. Adrenaline kicked in and he scrambled upwards like a madman into a strangler fig tree.

Lightning crackled above the canopy. Thunder rolled. Trees waved. No other athletes were in sight. Within minutes there was a foot of water on the Rainforest floor. The tree bark was slippery. The temperature plunged. He started to shiver. It was so dark. His thoughts about his uncle were unrepeatable.

Hugging the trunk he struggled to look at his luminous watch. Thank goodness the trainer had insisted that he wear one so he could pace himself and not burn out too soon. It was eleven o'clock in the morning but felt like midnight.

For one long hour he clung to the tree and then, as quickly as it had arrived, the floodwater subsided, leaving behind it a slimy mess along with some fish flopping about.

Darnley slithered down the tree and paddled his way back to the quagmire that was the Log Road. Other runners emerged from the Rainforest and squelched their way up the slope. The sun came out and steam rose from the jogging bodies. Soon, each athlete had a column of mosquitoes travelling above them like a frantic, vertical, black halo. Over the brow of the hill they jogged to find, to their surprise, a van selling some kind of burgers.

The downpour had robbed Darnley of energy and, as his knee was playing up a bit after the hill climb, temptation called. He slowed his pace and held out his hands to show that he had no cash with him. The van owner dismissed the gesture and insistently beckoned him over, handing him a burger in a bun, and then indicated that he should turn around so that he could slap a big plastic sticker on his back to advertise his business.

Joggers around him ignored the van and passed the munching Darnley with looks of disdain and the odd smirk. He gave the man a thumbs-up and set off again. When he glanced back he saw that one or two others were tempted as well and so he didn't feel too bad. The burger was even surprisingly good.

About seven kilometres further along the track, he felt decidedly uncomfortable in the stomach region but he persevered. The finish was only twelve kilometres away. He could make it. A further four kilometres though and he had abdominal cramps and was hauling himself along clutching his front. Then he was staggering in pain. One of the race supervisors cycled up beside him, struggling to keep his wheels straight in the sludge.

'You OK, sirrrrr?' he enquired in a heavy accent.

'Fine. Fine.' He summoned a smile. 'I've just got a little cramp.'

'I stay with you. Yes?'

'No. Go on. I'm alright.' He waved the man away. It was time for a dive into the undergrowth.

When Darnley came out again, he felt marginally better but far from well. He struggled on with wobbly legs, panting in the heat. He had slowed to an unsteady walk. Three kilometres to go. Now he was limping. A feeling of unreality took over, a suspension of time and space, a dreamlike world in which he ran but was not really part of it.

He heard cheering. Up ahead, the track shimmered with a mirage. Beyond it, distorted crowds waved, hooted and whistled. The finish was in sight. Various national flags fluttered from the trees. With all the grace of a drunken giraffe, Darnley staggered about until he finally tripped over and fell face down in the orange coloured mud. Groaning, he hauled himself onto all fours and crawled onto the mat.

'You have to stand up on it,' the managing supervisor said, somewhat shocked by the runner's appearance which was somewhere between a spectre and a mud skipper but he helped him to his feet. 'We've extended the cut-off because of the heavy rainfall,' he said.

The machine printed out Darnley's time. It wasn't very good; ten hours, five minutes and forty-one seconds. Never mind, he had finished. He had raised his million pounds for charity. Uncle's inheritance would be his. Then everything went black.

*

In the men's ward of the little local hospital, the triumphant but completely worn out athlete looked at the canula and drip in his arm.

'Ah. You arrr awake now,' a kindly nurse said, taking his wrist in her cool hands for a pulse check. 'Docterrrr will be with you in a momento.'

The doctor arrived. He was German. 'You haf hat a nasty case of foot poisoning.'

'Foot poisoning?' Darnley queried. His feet felt sore but nothing more.

'Yes. You haf eaten some bad meat.'

Darnley understood and nodded. 'It must have been that burger.'

'It vos not a goot idea to eat snake-burger from a vayside van.'

*

Fully recovered and back in England, the jubilant Darnley bounced up the stairs to the solicitor's office. He'd had a call to say to come in. The letter from the Amazon Log Road Marathon committee had obviously arrived. The fortune was within his grasp. The secretary showed him in.

The solicitor stood up and came around to the client's side of the big mahogany desk.

'Take a seat, dear boy. I have some news for you.'

Darnley sat down, grinning, rubbing the palms of his hands together in lascivious anticipation.

'You'd better read this.'

Blood drained from Darnley's face. It couldn't be true. All that training, the blisters, the knee, the flood, mosquito bites and food-poisoning, the struggle to the finish...

'Yes, they seem to have disqualified you,' the solicitor said noncommittally. I think, if you look at the bottom of the letter, it says something about Clause 15, subsection 25ii. I took the liberty of downloading the rules from the Internet.'

'And?'

'It seems that eating from anywhere but a designated refreshment point during the marathon results in automatic disqualification. I'm terribly sorry, dear boy. Never mind, you can always try again next year.'

Jump to it!

'I'm never going to beat them, those East European high-jumpers. They're as thin as rakes and fly through the air like grasshoppers.'

'Ah,' said his trainer conspiratorially shaking a white, cardboard shoebox at him, 'this year is going to be different.'

Craig looked up from his dejected slump on the changing room bench. 'How?'

'With these.' The trainer whipped the lid from the box to display a pair of spiked, lime-green, high-jump shoes nestling in tissue paper.

'I can't wear those. I'll be a laughing stock,' the youth protested, shaking his head from side to side at the very idea.

'Just try them on. They're your size. I had them made especially.'

'Oh, alright. Just to please you but I'm not wearing them in the competition.'

The trainer folded his arms and stood back approvingly as Craig put them on, tied the laces and stood up.

'They feel different.'

'That's because they are. Try jumping up and down gently.'

The lad did so and rose into the air so fast and high that he nearly hit his head on the lamp above. Panicking, he shouted, 'How do I stop?' for he was bouncing around the locker room like a space-hopper. The trainer pointed a remote control at the shoes and Craig came down with a thud.

'Where did you get them? They're fantastic.'

'My lips are sealed,' said the trainer, 'but they didn't come cheaply.'

Craig sat down, unlaced one shoe, took it off and inspected it closely. 'Apart from the revolting colour, they don't look or feel any different from my normal spiked trainers.'

'That is the secret of their success. They conform to the sole maximum thickness of 13 millimetres and the heel of 19 millimetres.'

'But I can't go bouncing along like this during the run-up,' Craig said sceptically. 'I'll look like a dolphin!'

'No, no. You don't understand. I'll switch the shoes on with this remote control just as your take-off foot hits the ground.'

'We'll need to practise that where we can't be seen.'

'No problem. I've got just the right place. My back garden. It's very secluded.'

*

It was the day of the final. Craig double-tied his laces for safety. Trainer and competitor had perfected the technique. The remote control beam was adjusted so that it wasn't as strong for the heats and Craig sailed convincingly through to the finals. Nine other competitors had made it and the East Europeans were looking smug.

The beep sounded. Craig crouched slightly and then, beginning with his take-off foot, ran his five straight paces parallel to the bar before starting the curve, hitting his white marker on the ground as he built up speed and momentum in the next five paces to give him the best possible take-off.

Favouring the two-arm pump action designed to propel him swiftly upwards, he gave it his all and, as his shoulders cleared the lowest central point of the bar, he threw his head back, put his hands down to his thighs and arched his back. As soon as his hips were over, he tucked his chin in, kicked his legs up and then, triumphantly threw his arms and then his legs out wide as he coasted down to land on the other side on his upper back on the lovely soft cushions.

Notch by notch the bar went up as the East Europeans dropped out until, finally, only Craig and one of their number were left to battle it out. If ever there was a gladiatorial spirit, this was it. Back and forth they ran and jumped. The crowd went wild. The world record was broken three jumps ago. The trainer turned up the beam strength.

Craig felt a buzzing in his right take-off foot. As he hit the white marker, ran the last five curved strides and launched himself upwards, gliding effortlessly over the bar, a unified gasp came from all around the arena. He drifted down and hit the cushions with a satisfying flumph. It was only then that he realised that sparks were coming out of the heel of his right shoe and that he had left a trail in the air like a rocket on firework night. He lay there, struggling to untie the double knot but his fingers were sweaty and he couldn't get a grip. He urgently tugged at the heel but his laces were firmly fixed. The sparks set fire to the landing cushions which started to smoulder with an acrid and breath-taking stench. The television cameras zoomed in to capture the drama.

'Somebody help me! Help me!'

The trainer stuffed the remote controller into his pocket, leapt over the barrier and pounded across the grass as Craig manoeuvred himself backwards in crab fashion, screaming 'Get it off me!' The timekeeper called for first aid and fire fighters on his phone. With one almighty wrench that nearly dislocated Craig's ankle, the trainer pulled the shoe off violently and hurled it across the turf where it smouldered and turned over like a dying crackerjack..

'It was all his idea,' sobbed the distraught athlete, kneeling as he tried to haul himself up. 'He made me do it.' Then he took a swipe at the trainer's solar plexus but the man saw it coming and swerved so that the impact hit his tracksuit trousers pocket... and the remote. Clinging to him, Craig pulled himself up onto his good foot, gave a little shuffle to get his balance before having another go at striking the man, and consequently left the ground by a good metre. 'Aaaaah!' he yelled as he shot upwards, and 'Aaaaah!' again as he ricocheted up and down on the spot. He was last seen hopping in kangaroo size bounds over the stadium's perimeter wall.

The three East Europeans took their places on the podium, clutched bouquets of flowers, shed tears as their flag was raised and went home jubilant. Craig was hopping mad.

Team Spirit.

Mr. Plewett, managing director of Plewett Sports, the nation-wide sports shop chain, appeared on the monitors at the daily videoconference.

'Friends,' he said with a benevolent smile to his managers, 'it is my pleasure to announce a new incentive designed to promote team spirit. This year, on the very last Sunday in the month of May, we are going to stage an employees' pentathlon. Single sex teams of five may enter for the following sports: hurdles, javelin, discus, relay and putting the shot. The event will take place in the Trethelean Stadium in Worcestershire. The winners, one team of men and one of women, will benefit from an all expenses paid holiday for themselves and a guest each at one of our luxury Mediterranean sports resorts. Those in training may use our unparalleled training facilities at off-peak times. Thank you for your attention. Don't forget that fitness and health are our watchwords.'

There was a 'bing-bong' and the screen went blank.

Mandy cashed up behind the counter in the local outlet. It had been a typical Saturday, full of time-wasters, smelly feet, badly behaved youngsters and one half-hearted shop-lifter.

'Put the door blind down, please, will you Carole? Oh, and flip the CLOSED sign over, ta.' Her second in command did so and then came across to lean against the glass-topped counter.

'Did you see that notice on the staff-room board?'

'Seven thousand, two hundred and eight-five pounds and forty pence,' she replied.

'Not bad,' Carole commented,' but did you hear what I said?'

Mandy put the takings in the reinforced bag and dropped it into the time-lock safe under the floor. Security would pick them up on Monday morning. 'Yes, I heard. You mean that competition for the luxury holiday? It only came through yesterday. Do you want to have a go?'

'It'd be fun.'

'How fit are you and what about the others? We need five of us. You and I are built for strength rather than speed.'

'I've already talked to the two Saturday girls and they're up for it.'

'We need one more.'

The door to the workroom upstairs slammed shut and the click of stiletto heels came pedantically down the curved wooden staircase. Mrs. Summerton had finished for the day in her grotto of sewing machines, mannequins and ironing boards. It was there that she wove her magic, creating tennis dresses, swimsuits and bespoke tee-shirts and tracksuits for those who didn't conform to stock sizes or who wanted something a little bit different.

'Ah, there you are,' said Mandy to the tall, elegant and somewhat genteel lady of a certain age and even more uncertain means. 'Did you see the notice about the pentathlon?'

'Indeed I did, Mandy. Are you thinking of entering?'

'Yes, we are but we need one more for our team. How about you?'

'Oh, I couldn't possibly! I'm extremely busy.'

Carole sauntered over to her. 'You'd like a nice all expenses paid holiday, wouldn't you?'

'Well, yes, of course. Now you come to mention it, I think my husband would benefit too.'

'You do have an air of sportiness about you, if you don't mind me mentioning it,' Mandy chipped in, locking the till. Mrs. Summerton dimpled as far as her thin face would allow.

'I did rather excel at hurdles at school,' she mused, 'but that was a long time ago.'

'Oh go on! Say you'll do it! We can use the management training facilities.'

The older lady sucked in her cheeks and contemplated past glories.

'Very well. You've talked me into it,' she smiled.

*

'We look great in these,' Mandy said, looking down at her own outfit and those of the rest of her five-strong team.

'You've done a neat job, Mrs. Summerton.' They were all wearing shorts and tee-shirts in strawberry pink with sparkling, embossed logos on their chests stating, 'We'll win.'

'If hard work and dedication have anything to do with it, we should do well. My husband's been complaining about how many hours we have been putting in,' she laughed, casting her eyes around the Trethelean Sports Stadium. It wasn't quite as grand as it sounded, having been relinquished by a football team that had moved to a better venue several years ago. However, despite its shabbiness, it was adequate and there was something glorious about the acoustics and the sight of friends and family ensconced in the stands. The managing director's voice came over the loudspeakers on that fine May morning.

'It gives me great pleasure to declare the Plewett Sports empire games open. Fitness and health are our watchwords.' A cheer went up.

It was quite a day, packed with activity as the various teams progressed through the heats, leaping over hurdles, passing the baton, hurling the discus, heaving the shot and throwing the javelin. Employees from all over the country had been training for weeks, all intent on winning. Despite her maturity Mrs. Summerton had come up trumps and the Saturday girls were very quick on their feet over hurdles and in the relay. The more strongly built Mandy and Carole were in their element with the other items. Everybody had to take part in everything, but there was no doubt about it, the strengths pulled up the scores.

*

The sun beat down on the terrace next to the pool as the group luxuriated on sun-beds in the bliss that only a Mediterranean holiday can provide.

'Are you alright, my dear?' asked Mrs. Summerton of her husband who, wearing a Panama hat and outrageously jolly shirt over his Bermuda shorts, sat beside her, utterly and completely relaxed.

'Wonderful! How clever of you all to win this for us.'

The rest of the team lounged back contentedly. The Saturday girls' boyfriends were playing an impromptu game of water polo in the azure pool with Mandy's and Carole's partners.

'I'd love to go in for a swim,' Mandy said, lifting her arm that was encased in plaster from wrist to shoulder and nodding her head towards the tempting blue and sparkling water.

'Me too,' Carole said, tapping the cast on her left ankle.

'So would we, wouldn't we?' one of the Saturday girls said sadly, tentatively moving her head from side to side above the neck brace. Her friend grinned back with some pain, for the side of her face was the colour of a dark plum and her wrist bore a crepe bandage.

'It had all gone so well,' Mandy said with a deep sigh. 'One minute everything was OK. We'd won the prize, got the trophy and were happily singing in the showers...'

'You didn't mean to drop your soap on the floor...' said Carole.

'It really was an accident that I fell over you when you slipped on it...' Mandy said.

'... And we shouldn't have been running like that...' added one of the Saturday girls.

A waiter approached and handed a leaflet to each of them.

'We hope that you ladies will be able to come tonight,' he said in a charming French accent, as he passed on to the next group.

Mandy picked up the leaflet. 'It's for free drinks and a disco!' she shrieked with laughter.

'I don't think we'll be able to make it,' Carole said with mirth. 'We're already plastered!'

In the Swim

The indoor swimming pool was such an exciting place. For a mere tuppence it was possible to sit in the balconies that ran along both sides of the main bath. The whole building was stiflingly hot and stank of chlorine. The echo was deafening, the vaulted ceiling reverberating with the screeches of triumphant lemmings as they hurled themselves from the top diving board, plunged into the vivid blue water and surfaced to shake their hair like a mop. They'd strike forth towards the side, clamber out and then repeat the whole performance.

Dora sat there enthralled and full of admiration. How she longed to fly through the air, swim like a dolphin, plunge into the mysterious depths of the deep end and then go home on the bus with a towel rolled under her arm as if to declare to the world that she too was a swimmer.

Her dream was about to come true for, one day, mother said they were going swimming. She could hardly wait to get there. When they arrived in the changing room they undressed and put their clothes in a wire basket. Each person was given a rubber bracelet bearing their basket number. Tight rubber hats went on with chinstraps that strangled you and earflaps that cut out ninety percent of the sound. Then, off they tiptoed, along a dim corridor, into the freezing cold foot bath, under the shower and through the entrance that led onto the very narrow and slippery tiled edge that ran around the pool.

It was very busy with people of all ages splashing, ploughing through the water and submerging only to come up like blowing whales. The activities were peppered with the periodic sharp, piercing sound of the attendant's whistle as some boy misbehaved and was pointed at in admonishment.

Indeed, some were even told to get out of the pool if their antics were too rough.

However, here was Dora in her chain-store swimsuit in rouched turquoise and blue with her yards of long hair stuffed into the white rubber helmet so that she looked like a Martian, ready to take on the world of water. Mother got in first and coaxed her down the vertical wooden steps into the shallow end. That's where she spent part of a happy afternoon, clinging to the tiled side gully, doing the leg strokes and cringing when a wave came her way. All was going well until a shriek of horror came from her mother whose lovingly hand-crafted, knitted swimwear was stretching uncontrollably. The bikini bottom, dragged down by the weight of the water was slithering over her hips, destined for disaster, as she clutched at it with one hand and tried to stuff her attributes back into the top which was now resembling two string shopping bags.

'Out!' she said. 'Quickly! Out!'

'Aw, Mum...'

'Did you hear what I said?'

So that was that.

Time marched on and, in her tenth year, swimming lessons were mandatory at Dora's junior school. So, off they all trolled through the town in crocodile fashion and presented themselves in a row at the shallow end where a pushy instructor expected them to jump into the water and put their heads under when he pointed at each in turn. As the moment of dread came along the row towards her she slunk out of the pool via the steps, ran along behind him and slid in gently at the other side. There began a career in swimming avoidance which shadowed her school days in a welter of excuse-me notes containing everything from influenza to a sprained ankle.

By the end of senior school, Nora was the only person in the entire upper half of the establishment who could not swim. Despite being hauled across the shallow end on a rope, floated in a lorry tyre and bullied mercilessly by the portly little lady swimming teacher, she resolutely refused to take her feet off the bottom of the pool without some form of reliable support.

Then love struck.

'Come in for a swim,' said the hazel-eyed Adonis with the hairy chest and golden curls. The Lido, if only for sunbathing, was a great place for meeting boys at weekends. She looked up at him. He was quite a catch.

'I don't like the water,' she replied.

'You can't swim, can you?' he cajoled, having watched her from a distance the previous weekend..

'I could if I wanted to,' she said defiantly.

'Let me help you.'

'I'll think about it.'

'I'll kiss you underwater if you learn to swim,' he said as he flung his towel over his shoulder and swaggered off to the changing rooms.

Dora lay awake for half of the night trying to overcome her fear of the water. Oh, to be kissed by him! Underwater! How romantic, like a mermaid. She would let her long hair float about as he took her in his arms and administered the kiss from heaven.

The next day she was at the Lido early but he was nowhere to be seen. She changed into her lilac bikini and sat on the edge of the shallow end, dangling her feet in the tepid water. Not many people were about yet. She looked around anxiously. Suddenly he was beside her.

'Ready?' He slid into the water and held out his hand. She

took it and joined him. 'Now,' he said, 'this is what I suggest. I'm going to walk slowly backwards in front of you while you do the breast-stroke.'

'Oh I couldn't do that. There'd be nothing to stop me from sinking.'

'Well,' he said, a trifle flirtatiously, 'I was going to suggest that you only do part of the arm movement, allowing me to stand really close to you with my arms stretched forward.'

'That's outrageous"' she exclaimed. 'If I sank your hands would be... you know. Absolutely not!'

'Go on. Be a devil. Isn't it worth the risk?'

She looked at him standing there, sun glinting off his hairy arms, his curly eyelashes fringing those sexy hazel eyes.

'Very well,' she said, 'but if I start to sink you are only to put your hands under my chin.'

'Of course,' he said with a wicked grin. He hoped she would sink. Two minutes passed.

'I can't believe it,' Dora exclaimed, standing waist-deep and looking behind her at the expanse of pool she had swum across. 'I actually swam. Really swam!' The fear of her body sinking into those waiting hands had kept her going. She was incandescent with delight.

'What about our bargain,' the boy asked.

'I don't understand.' In the massive excitement of actually swimming, she had forgotten her motivation, the underwater kiss.

'My kiss.' Suddenly she was shy. She had never been kissed before.

'Come on,' he said, taking her by the hand and leading her across to the edge. 'Nobody's looking. Are you ready to go under?' She hated the thought of the water closing over her head, the sounds becoming muffled and not being able to breathe, but a kiss from Adonis, underwater, was something to remember all her life, and she did.

He took both her wrists and pulled her towards him, gazing tenderly into her eyes. Then his hands crept up her arms to the elbows as the two became even closer.

'Take a deep breath,' he said.

At the end of school term swimming sports, eighteen year old Dora had put her name down for the beginners' width. She lined up nonchalantly in the shallow end with a row of twelve-year-olds. She could swim and she would show them.

'Peep!' went the swimming teacher's whistle and Dora lunged forward, creating a bow-wave so vast that the beginners were swamped as she ploughed across to the other side, leaving the rest way behind. She stood up triumphantly, fists in the air, to the sound of clapping.

She thought of last weekend and how Adonis had taken her beneath the water. She had filled her lungs with air, closed her eyes and sunk down. His arms had encircled her and his lips found hers... and lost them... and found them again... and lost them. It was utterly impossible to get a grip with wet lips. He had held her tightly, fighting to get good facial orifice contact but the rubbery slippage was just too much. She had pushed him away as she surfaced gasping for air.

'That was awful,' she snapped, making for the steps out of the pool. 'It was like kissing an eel. I'm going to get changed.'

Scroll forward ten years. 'Come on, Jessie! You can do it!' Dora stood beside her daughter in the pool as the little girl splashed gamely forward, chin in the air.

'Oh well done! Look, Daddy's waving to you. He saw.'

'Daddy, I can swim!'

He came over. 'There's a clever girl.'

Dora smiled at them both. How the pool water glinted off their curly eyelashes!

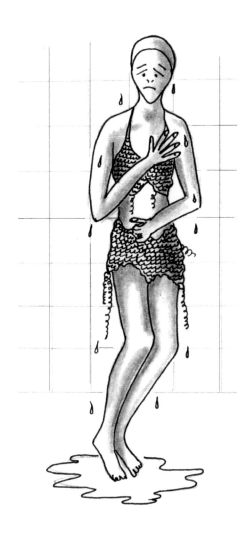

Sanchez

I owe everything Sanchez. Starting from that cold, rainy evening three years ago when he picked me up outside the cinema, invited me home and gave me supper and a bed for the night, we've never looked back. In these cynical times I know it's hard to believe but it really was love at first sight... a mutual understanding and respect that I had never known before. All my life I'd been treated like a nothing. I don't even know who my parents are, so to spend my days and nights with Sanchez is truly wonderful and I'm forever grateful.

He's a writer, based here in Brightlestone-on-Sea, who works from home providing copy about sports events for some Spanish newspaper. This fits in well with his other passion, me! No, I don't really mean that. Sanchez is an athlete. He runs. His speciality is the one hundred metres and he is second to best national record holder. It has irked him enormously that his main rival, Diego, also Spanish, keeps pipping him at the post by nanoseconds, but this season Sanchez has been utterly determined to outsmart him and win. I fully support his ambitions.

You could say that I live off Sanchez. Yes, I do. I contribute nothing whatsoever to the household financially but my input is beyond price. I suppose I should feel bad about this but I don't somehow. Well, he never makes me feel as if I'm scrounging. No, never. I know that I'm his inspiration and that just having me around all the time makes him feel calm and hopeful. He looks forward to seeing me when he wakes every morning. If he gets writer's block, he only has to look at me to find the words to keep on writing. All this is very flattering, of course. As I don't have any relatives to criticise my lifestyle, it doesn't matter at all and we just go on sweetly from day to day, him jabbering away in Spanish of which I comprehend not a single word. I'll never learn it but somehow it doesn't matter because we understand each other. He doesn't appear to speak any English at all although he seems to get the message about everything to do with his sport.

In the afternoons we often go to the park or walk into town but a jog along the promenade is my favourite. No matter what the weather... and this resort can be pretty breezy... there's nothing better than the smell of the sea, powering in from the blue-grey horizon as the waves crash onto the shingle. We come home smelling of the ocean with the taste of salt on our tongues and flop out on the sofa and fall asleep together, me in his arms.

One afternoon we are dozing after such an outing and the doorbell rings. Blearily, Sanchez gets up and goes to answer. It's Diego. Although they're rivals they are also great friends but I can't stand the guy with his goggly eyes and habit of breaking into mock sparring. When I hear his voice in the hall, I drag myself through into the bedroom and continue my nap on the bed. Sanchez and Diego start rattling off in Spanish in the other room but I just drown it out with thoughts of swimming in the sea.

It's dark when I wake up later and the flat is quiet. They've gone out. I'm pretty miffed because I don't like being left out like that but I suppose they didn't want to wake me. The television is on standby so I go back to the sofa, hit the remote 'on' button and watch some banal programme or other. It's lonely without Sanchez.

He comes home late, alone and smelling of fish and chips. I give him a reproachful look.

In the morning we're up early again and take to the road in companionable silence. Plod, plod, plod... the sound of trainers hitting the tarmac. He gives me a look and a smile and my heart turns over. All is OK with us again. I love this guy. We work our way along the country lanes, past the fields of sheep and horses, past the farm and the smell of manure and hay, up onto the hilltop where we stop, panting, to enjoy a panoramic view of the English Channel below us. There are some boats on the horizon and the waves are breaking out on the sandbank.

'Hermosa,' Sanchez says, gazing out at the view, but I don't know what it means. Just living in the moment with him is enough. We sit down together on the lush, green turf and rest for a while. He puts his arm around me. There are common blue butterflies on this chalk downland and we watch them flitting about, pausing momentarily on the clover but never stopping for more than a few seconds. It's quite idyllic and I could stay here forever in the warm, morning sun, with the sea glinting and the scent of the grass.

Next morning, Sanchez decides to go to the gym for a workout. I'm not keen on these indoor training sessions and he knows it so I stay at home and have a relaxing morning in the garden. The kids next door are noisy and their mother keeps yelling at them. I can see the washing on the line and hear the squeak of the swing going back and forth, back and forth. Why on Earth don't they oil it? It really stresses my ears. I just put up with it though in a spirit of neighbourliness. Then one of the children starts screaming about something. It's grim trying to ignore it. I sigh deeply and try to count my blessings. It's better living here than anywhere else I've ever been.

Sanchez comes home smelling deliciously of perspiration. I just love the scent of his fresh sweat and he greets me with a smile, jabbers something in Spanish and goes into the shower. Diego comes round again later and they more or less ignore me as they sit poring over charts and checking each other's pulses and blood pressures on one of those home kits. It's always like this before a big race. They don't have time for anything or anybody. The race is everything.

So the next day we all pile into Diego's old car and head for the stadium. They always put me in the back, which I hate, but it's his car and we have to comply. Anyway, the two guys like to sit together in the front, chatting away in Spanish as I just look out of the window, watching the world go by, observing the other traffic. I always go with Sanchez. I'm his lucky charm and today I think positive thoughts, willing him to overtake the pompous Diego and carry off the trophy. I can just imagine it now, standing on our mantle-piece.

Half-way there the car starts playing up. There's a sort of spluttering noise and it grinds to a halt on a roundabout... not the best of places. So the boys get out and push it to the side of the road. There's a lot of honking from other motorists. I keep well out of that sort of thing and just stay sitting aloof in the back, pretending that this embarrassing occurrence has nothing whatsoever to do with me and that I usually ride in much better vehicles than this one.

Diego calls the rescue service on his mobile phone. There's a wait of an hour and they are both getting edgy. It's hot in the car but I stay there while they lean against the outside. When the mechanic arrives, Diego speaks to him in English, which surprises me somewhat. I hear phrases like 'Dirt in the carburettor' and 'It looks like your oil needs changing'. Then we're underway again, frantically trying to make up time.

When we arrive at the stadium we park up. They get their gear out of the boot. The security guard is temporarily away from the competitors' entrance that bears a sign saying 'Competitors Only' and we rush through to the changing rooms. They are empty. Everybody is out on the track or doing field events or, if they've already done their stint, watching from the raised seats. Sanchez and Diego get into their running clothes and shoes with spikes on. I'm going to stay in the changing rooms, as usual. I can't bear to watch the actual race. Sanchez says something to me, kisses me on the top of my head and waves to me as he goes out with a tense smile. They exchange some words of banter and shove each other in playful fashion in the doorway. Then they are gone.

I pace backwards and forwards in the echoing room. There are tracksuits, shoes and shorts everywhere. I can't settle. I know this race is important to him. I desperately want him to beat that beastly Diego. The sound of cheering comes in through the high, pebble-glass windows. My curiosity gets the better of me and I climb up onto the bench and try and look out of the windows but they are too high up. I climb down. No, I mustn't watch. It might be unlucky for him.

The changing room door opens. A security guard stares at me with hostility.

'What are you doing in here?' he asks. I don't wait but rush past him and out into the bright sunshine.

'Come back!' he shouts after me but I don't. I run around the outside of the building and find my way into the dimly lit tunnel that leads under the stands to the sports arena. I'm panting but he won't catch me. This time, yes, this time, just for once I'm going to see Sanchez win. As I get nearer to the tunnel exit, the hollow echoes of my own sounds meld with the cacophony of tooting, cheering and thumping coming in from outside.

I break out into the sunshine again. Loudspeakers are blaring. There's a big, illuminated scoreboard at each end of the field area. In the middle of it, I can see endless activity. People are running and then jumping into the sandpit. Others are leaping over bars. I pause, not sure where to go. Ahead, a discus whizzes through the air. Around the edge, on the track, runners in the ten thousand metres relay are strung out like a string of pearls. I spot the finishing line. That's where I need to be.

'Men's one hundred metres final, in two minutes time,' the announcer says. The sound reverberates all around the stadium and I hear, 'time... time... time...' fading away. It's all so exciting.

Trying to look nonchalant I edge my way along in front of the barrier and quietly saunter towards to the finish where I can see a sign that says, '100 metres. FINISH.' That's it. I'm progressing quite well when I hear a shout behind me as two security guards rush up and try to grab me.

'Come along, fella-me-lad. You know you're not allowed here.'

I ignore them and break into a trot. I am determined to see Sanchez win. I hear a starting pistol, look over my shoulder, and sure enough, the one hundred metres race is underway. The runners are streaming down the track towards me but I want to be there at the finish before them so I put a spurt on and arrive there ready to greet Sanchez as he comes over the finishing line. It all goes wrong somehow, though. In my excitement I rush forward too soon into his arms and the tightly knit group of runners trip over each other and fall into disarray. Sanchez doubles up, the others hit the deck and that redoubtable Diego prances over the finishing line with a look of surprise and smugness on his face.

'Perro tento!' Sanchez shouts, pushing me away as I try to lick his face.

I don't understand. Why isn't he pleased to see me?

'Is this your dog?' demands a panting security man.

Lucky for Some

'Now, now!' said Alice. 'Just you stop licking yourself or you'll get those disgusting fur-balls again!' She lifted the plump, black cat from the sun-baked windowsill and placed him on the curly-cut rug in front of the bare fireplace of her small sewing room. He let out a muted yowl of disapproval and looked questioningly up at her with his luminous, amber eyes.

She took a bright yellow duster from her apron pocket and methodically wiped up the hairs that the cat had left behind. How she hated the constant mess and dirt-boxes, not to mention his sensitive stomach and the claw-damage to her carpets and doors! However, she cared for Lucky because he was her husband's love-object and, by keeping the cat happy, she kept her husband contented and, let it be said, she held onto her husband, knowing for years that the marriage was dead and one day, when Lucky was gone, Jack would go too.

'Time for milk?' she queried. The cat followed her into the large kitchen. As usual, the big, over-fed tom entwined himself in and out of her legs as she stooped to get out a bottle of full-cream gold-top. The purring at the prospect of his daily delight rivalled the hum of the fridge in amplitude. 'There,' she said, passing her hand perfunctorily over his sleek head. He lapped contentedly until the saucer was shiny clean.

*

The evening news was just as always... a war somewhere, a royal visit and an unwanted road scheme. The weather forecast was 'changeable'. Jack sat dozing in his chair. The huge black cat was curled up asleep on his master's lap, whiskers drooping, sides heaving as he breathed steadily. The evening newspaper had slipped onto the floor and Jack's spectacles sat crookedly on his red, thread-veined nose. The empty wineglass glinted by the light of the table-lamp and his many golf trophies winked from cabinets around the room. Alice put down her knitting and shuffled through to make the bedtime drink. Her husband heard the click of the kettle switch and, spluttering, came out of his nap, grumbling that he'd missed the news again and why hadn't she woken him?

He fondled Lucky's sleek coat lovingly and spoke sweet nothings to his furry friend. The cat awoke and gazed up adoringly into his face and shuddered a contented sigh.

'Did you cook his plaice, Alice?' Jack demanded.

'Yes dear,' his wife said patiently.

'It's fresh today, isn't it?' he checked.

'Of course dear,' she replied automatically.

'What will you give him tomorrow?'

'I thought a little rainbow trout.'

'Has he had chicken lately?'

'He'll have that the day after.'

Discussions over Lucky's diet were the mainstay of the conversation. She always wanted to scream loudly, 'To hell with the flaming cat!' She had so wanted children… silk-cheeked children with blond hair like Jack's used to be … and with shining hazel eyes and arms that would hug your neck… not claw-tagged pads that would scratch you if you didn't watch out… but now it was too late.

It had been a mid-life romance when bachelor bank manager Jack had suddenly courted his long-time secretary Alice, after his aged mother had died. Everyone had been taken by surprise when he'd lavished Alice with red roses, gift-wrapped presents and cosy dinners in expensive restaurants. At first the mousy spinster had been very coy, simpering as she shuffled in and out of the manager's office, her blushing countenance shielded by a sheaf of papers, for all the world like a Geisha girl. How often then had he buzzed her on the intercom and, in a voice husky with promise, invited her to 'come in for a little dictation'.

The 'IN CONFERENCE' sign had gone up on the outside of the office door and raised eyebrows and knowing winks had been the order of the day. The middle-aged bride-to-be had basked in her hour of glory. Wedding presents grew in stacks upon her normally tidy desk as female staff spent lunch-hours leafing through 'bridey' magazines and lingerie catalogues.

Out went her dull, grey suits and sensible shoes. In came fetching two-pieces with lively blouses. Lunch-hours were extended for yet another experimental hairstyle. When the bridegroom elect came upon the twittering crowd of women in this hitherto staid and solemn bank, his fly-away eye-brows shot up in mock surprise and the gaggle of girls scattered like autumn leaves to let the engaged couple be alone in the staff-room.

The wedding arrangements had been lavish but formal. There were no relatives, just senior bank staff and Jack's golf cronies, an exit from the registry office in a shower of confetti and a dash through an arch of golf clubs held aloft by his friends. The bride, incandescent with delight in a peach confectionary suit and meringue hat, embarked on the world of marriage, clinging to the arm of her new husband's tailored suit.

Alice simply glowed. Her cup ran over with happiness at this mid-life romance that had suddenly blossomed for a woman who had adored her boss from a-far for years. The reception, held in the Orchid Suite of the most up-market hotel in town, was discreetly extravagant, with oysters, smoked salmon and strawberries and cream, enjoyed to the music of an elegant string quartet.

After the honeymoon in the Bahamas, Alice did not return to the bank but whole-heartedly threw herself into the role of wife. Despite an irrational wish to become a mother, life was sweet. Her dreams of parenthood foundered on double rocks, however, for nature had cruelly closed the door on her chance of motherhood and her new husband had locked it with indifference.

Overnight, Prince Charming became a cold and unloving figure who spurned his new wife's craving for affection. He came home one evening bearing a small black kitten.

'Mew,' it cried. Alice took it into her neat little hands.

'Mew,' it went.

'That should keep you busy!' said Jack, hanging up his coat and making for his favourite armchair and the newspaper. The loss of his mother had clearly indicated to him that a substitute housekeeper was needed. His middle-aged wife filled the role perfectly in the extended bungalow next to the golf course.

Fate, however, is a strange thing for Alice wasn't keen on cats and Jack found himself the object of the kitten's attention. They named it 'Lucky' and it waited for him on the front window-ledge and nestled on his lap in the evenings. It seemed to sense that here was an ally. As the kitten changed into a cat, an affectionate bond grew between them that excluded Alice who still passionately yearned for her callous husband.

On this late summer night, however, Alice brought the bedtime drinks into the sitting room, placing the tray on the little mosaic coffee table. Jack tenderly apologised to the black, fluffy beast on his lap and took up the mug of sweet beverage.

'There, there,' he said. 'Did Daddy disturb his poor, little Fluffumkins?' Lucky re-settled himself, casting a disdainful eye up at Jack sipping ceremoniously at his Coronation mug.

The years ticked by in a regular rhythm of domesticity. Alice lay on her back and contemplated the bedroom ceiling that was stippled with reflected light from the wet road outside. Jack snored. So did the cat. Alice wept. If she lost her husband, she would be so alone but she was lonely now even though they were together. He lived for his work, his golf and his cat. She lived for him, alone and trapped in her misery.

The next day was Saturday. A pearly pink dawn saw Alice waving and watching her husband go off as usual, wearing his moss-green jacket and checked cap, carrying his golf-bag and a spare five-iron over his shoulder. He was a fine figure of a man, despite his forthcoming retirement. Who would have believed that he'd find the energy to play cricket on Sunday too?

'A shame he can't find any time for me,' Alice cogitated grimly but quickly bethought herself. She had a nice home, a husband for public occasions and plenty of spare time. He wouldn't be back until late and the day was hers. She reached into her apron pocket and took out the list. Toilet rolls, vitamin tablets for the cat and denture powder. In the chemist's shop she hesitated before paying but then she remembered... the hair dye. This was an ideal opportunity to do it while he was away all day.

It was warm outside and the long walk home from the shops took its toll. Alice was relieved to sit down on the bentwood chair in her shady kitchen. How she hated the heat!

'Miaow,' said Lucky.

'Oh you wretched cat!' she snapped at him. 'Can't you see I'm hot and tired! Wait a moment!'

'Miaow,' he nagged.

Alice stood up irritably and made towards the fridge. She stooped and took out the milk bottle just as Lucky slid in between her ankles. In that split second of loss of balance and summer-heat whoosiness, over she went.

*

It was nearly midnight when Jack came whistling and weaving his way to the front door of his plush, suburban house. For once his devoted little wife wasn't standing waiting to release the latch at the sound of his erratic steps. So he fumbled for his key and let himself awkwardly into the dark, dumping his golf trolley in the corner.

He found her on the kitchen floor, a pool of rancid milk congealed about her matted hair and Lucky asleep on her chest. Jack was brought to sobriety very quickly indeed. Was she dead? He gently lifted the waking cat from the recumbent body of his wife and placed his own balding head against her chest. The heart was beating feebly. 'Wake up Alice!' he said but she didn't. He staggered to the 'phone to call an ambulance.

Three months later Alice came out of hospital in a wheelchair, having shown no pleasure at the prospect of coming home despite the cajoling of medical staff. The waxwork wife sat staring vacantly ahead with a tartan rug over her knees. Apart from eating and drinking, she hadn't been able to move since the fall. Not a word had passed her lips and there had been no sign that she could hear.

Jack, who had led an eminently selfish life, was not one to feed and wash an invalid, even though she was the wife who would have slavishly cared for him in similar circumstances. Oh no! The punishing and relentless round of caring was not for him! Agency nurses were employed day and night and a neighbour sat in during the early evening. His senior position at the bank had ensured plenty of cash to pay for this and, in any case, there was the insurance and his investments.

Life didn't really change much for Jack. He still fell asleep to the news and Alice's nurse made his bedtime drink. He continued to enjoy his golf and cricket weekends. He stroked his moustache at the thought of it. Oh yes! The games would go on! The only real difference in lifestyle was that now he and the cat had a double bed to themselves while Alice slept in her former sewing room. Otherwise things went on much as normal for him.

One evening, while he was sitting in the lounge with Lucky on his lap, tenderly stroking the cat's luscious fur and enjoying the soft, responsive purring, his pleasure was shattered by the night-nurse rushing into the room.

'Come quickly, Mr. Clark!' she insisted. 'Something's happened to your wife!'

Jack rose, still clinging to the cat and hurriedly walked through to Alice's bedroom. She was hanging out of bed, her limp body trailing towards the open bedside cupboard.

'There's no pulse,' said the night nurse. 'I'll call the doctor.' Jack tickled the cat under the chin and said calmly, 'Mummy's gone, Lucky.' Then he turned, walked out of the room and went back to turn on the news.

The night-nurse took out her box of cotton wool in preparation and rearranged Alice tidily on the bed while she waited for the doctor. Then she saw that the deceased woman was clutching something awkwardly in her hand. The nurse prised open the fist, took out the tube and put it back in the cupboard. These stroke patients got some funny ideas sometimes!

'Coronary thrombosis,' declared the doctor. 'A clot must have moved.' Jack nodded acceptingly. He stroked Lucky thoughtfully and went slowly out of the room. He ought to buy some fish.

The small group of neighbours and Jack's golfing friends around the graveside had come as a mark of respect for

Alice, for few of the former had any time for Jack. With his late nights at the office and his weekend golf and cricket, they knew how lonely his devoted wife had been - how frequently she had gently declined their many invitations to party-plan evenings, coffee mornings and shopping trips into town. The answer had always been the same. Jack was expecting her to have done this or that for him. He so enjoyed her home baking, the hand-laundered and expertly pressed shirts, the beautifully arranged flowers, hand-knitted diamond-patterned sweaters and scrupulously neat and tidy house. Those trophies took a lot of polishing too. Most of all, the cat couldn't be left for long. They all accepted her reasons. What else could they do? Now, however, Alice was dead. They all crowded into Jack's lounge and ate ham sandwiches and drank sherry, admired his golfing trophies, and looked through his cuttings book before sorrowfully taking their leave of the widower who held Lucky in his arms as he saw them out with a feeling of relief. It was all over and he was glad.

Now that his wife had departed this life, the nurses were no longer needed. It was just the man and his cat. In the evenings, the newly bereaved sat there, alone, in front of the television. Alice's knitting was still by her chair. Jack had consumed yet another take-away. He started to rhythmically stroke the cat. He took up the silver-backed, grooming brush and worked methodically through the long dark hair of the much-spoiled, over-fed moggie who purred his appreciation in insincere cadences.

Jack sat there, night after night, stroking and grooming Lucky. Maybe he was going mad but surely the cat was looking a bit different? At the end of four weeks a miracle happened. Lucky had changed colour from a luscious, rippling black to an orange and white ginger tom. Jack took him to the animal clinic.

'Perfectly healthy,' said the cheery Australian vet who prised open the cat's mouth and received a hiss. 'Yes, he's in very good condition. Bit over-weight. How long have you had him? About five years?'

Jack's mouth dropped open like a stunned fish. 'He... he's at least sixteen...sixteen,' he stammered.

The vet looked up. 'You're joking! This is a young cat.'

Whatever miracle had happened to change a black cat into a ginger tom and an old cat into a young one, Jack didn't know but when he eventually got around to clearing out his dead wife's bedroom, perhaps the penny dropped when he found, in the bedside cupboard, a pile of tubes of black hair dye...

Ribbons

'I don't wanna do it!'

'Aw honey, you know you don't mean that.'

Thirteen-year-old Dinah-Dee Gantrey stamped her small foot and pouted, looking resolutely at the floor. She was a force to be reckoned with in her turquoise, bejewelled leotard and her hair scraped up into a tight bun on top of her head.

'Momma's goin' to buy you a spankin' new, gold-plated bicycle when you win the acrobatic ribbon dancing. Jest think how lovely that silver cup will look in the cabinet... and your Daddy's goin' to be real proud of you.' Daddy was a millionaire stockbroker.

'You're not my Momma. My real Momma's dead and I hate you.'

Tears welled up in her eyes, threatening to smudge the carefully applied mascara and turquoise eye shadow. The trainer, Verity, stepped forward and placed her hand gently on the child's shoulder.

'Perhaps you should take your seat now, Mrs. Gantrey. She's on after the next one.'

'Yes, of course.' Then she turned to Dinah-Dee and said smarmily, 'Now, don't you forget to smile real wide. Here are your pretty, twirly ribbons, all nicely wound onto the sticks. Remember, crisp, clean finishes.' She bent over, putting her high, blonde, beehive hair-do at risk, and planted a wet and lipsticky kiss on the child's cheek. 'I'm gonna to take my seat now and watch ma little girl win. It's a real shame your Daddy can't be here. He's at another of those high-powered meetings of his.'

'I'm not your little...' but the woman had gone. The trainer threw a scowl at her back and turned to Dinah-Dee.

'Ready now?'

The child protégée nodded and said loudly, 'I wanna go to the rest-room.'

Equally loudly, the trainer replied, 'There isn't time. You should have gone before.'

'I need to go NOW!'

'Go on then but be very quick!' Verity folded her arms and leaned against the wall.

In her front row seat next to the display floor, Dinah-Dee's step-mother sat in a cloud of pungent perfume, immediately turning to the people on either side of her to explain loudly about her talented, ribbon-twirling, acrobatic daughter. 'She's double-jointed,' she said, 'and defies gravity.'

The listeners smiled patiently and nodded. Applause rang out as one competitor left the arena, only having dropped two points. Dinah-Dee's name and number were announced. She didn't appear. She was called again. Nothing.

Her step-mother bustled down the corridor on her way to the changing rooms. Verity, the trainer, met her halfway along.

'She's disappeared. We can't find her anywhere. The police have been called.'

Mrs. Gantrey went berserk.

Two days later, Dinah-Dee had not been found alive or dead. Then a ransom note was discovered attached to the big iron gates that guarded the entrance to the driveway of the North Fork estate.

'TWO MILLION DOLLARS OR SHE WILL DIE. AWAIT INSTRUCTIONS.' The writing was in big black capitals on file paper. The police fingerprinted it without success.

'Oh my poor baby!' Mrs. Gantrey was beside herself with mock grief. She detested the child and the feeling was mutual.

Next day, somebody handed in an envelope they had found tacked to a wooden telegraph pole just outside town. It was addressed to the Gantreys. Inside, it said:

'MR. GANTREY IS TO PLACE TWO MILLION DOLLARS IN USED $100 BILLS IN A BLACK RUCKSACK IN THE TRASH CAN OUTSIDE ELM HILL JUNIOR HIGH SCHOOL AT 3PM TOMORROW OR SHE WILL DIE.'

'We have to pay,' sobbed Mrs. Gantrey.

'Sure, honey. We'll pay.' Her husband comforted her, running his tongue over his lips to get rid of the taste of her hair lacquer as she howled on his shoulder. The police said reassuringly that they would have plain-clothes officers around the pick-up point to seize the kidnappers when they came to collect the ransom money and that there was a good chance that Dinah-Dee would be returned to the bosom of her family, safe and sound.

Next afternoon the deed was done as hundreds of pupils spilled out of the school and piled into buses. How it happened, nobody saw, but the rucksack and its contents disappeared and Dinah-Dee was never found.

Verity, her trainer, was so upset about the girl's disappearance that she discontinued training child acrobatic ribbon dancers and moved south to the Atlantic coast to open a surf-board shop. It's called *Surf you Right*. If you should be down that way anytime, it's well worth a look in. It's run by Verity and her brother and his daughter Celine.

Sometimes on moonlit evenings, Verity and Celine go down to the wide, sandy beach, take out their ribbon sticks and perform acrobatic dances, twirling and somersaulting to the relentless pounding of the waves. It has taken Dinah-Dee a while to get used to her new name.

Marooned

International blond tennis star Kurt Manners dried himself, threw the monogrammed towel onto a chair and surveyed his fine physique in the full-length changing room mirror at the All Countries Tennis Club. He patted the taught muscles of his drum-tight stomach, clenched his buttocks, pumped his biceps and stood sideways before the Adonis-like reflection smiling back at him.

The fans had been there as usual, clamouring to touch him as he'd climbed out of his Fersparti by the Members' entrance. Pop stars and their groupies? Forget it! Sport was where the adulation was!

Today was the first round of the annual prestigious tournament. He was Number One in the All Countries Tennis rankings and would sail through the draw. Already he could feel the cool, gold trophy pressed against his cheek as he, the winner, posed triumphantly for the photographers after the final.

During the championships, newspaper headlines would chart his success with increasing fervour from 'Kurt through first round!' to 'Charismatic Kurt Captures Cup!' ('and a nice big fat cheque for half a million pounds,' he muttered aloud to himself.)

'What did you say, man?' asked a deep voice. The poseur turned to face the short, stocky, black guy before him. He hastily reclaimed the towel and covered his crown jewels.

'Er - I was just thinking aloud about the draw. We meet this afternoon if rain holds off.' He took a step away from his opponent, Gizmo Bundi from Tanzabatia. He forced a stiff smile. 'Was there something you wanted?'

Gizmo grinned like a melon slice, stepped forward and slapped Kurt on the shoulder. 'No man. Just wanted to wish you luck! See you on court!' Then he left.

The nerve! To wish HIM luck, he, the champion for two years running! He turned his proud head and looked down his aquiline nose at the tainted shoulder.

The television commentator could hardly contain his amusement. 'Kurt's OUT! It's unbelievable! Wild card Gizmo Bundi of Tanzabatia has beaten the defending champion in three straight sets!' He turned to his companion in the courtside mini-studio. 'What do you say to that Patti?'

'Well, this really is unprecedented. Kurt has won every single grand slam this past year. His trainer assured me earlier today that this first-round match held no problems whatsoever for him. I can't imagine what went wrong. The players are coming off court and here comes Gizmo Bundi now. Congratulations Gizmo! You must be very pleased with your performance out there today.'

Gizmo pushed back his short, frizzy hair, pulled his sweaty sports shirt away from his chest, wiped his nose with the back of his hand and grinned up at the interviewer.

'Yes Ma'am! I sure was somethin' and that guy just don't know what hit him!' He cackled and shook with laughter.

Suddenly a loud crash interrupted them. They both turned to look off-camera. Patti hastily carried on, 'It seems that somebody has knocked over a flower pedestal. Well...' she hesitated.

'Wind up!' said the producer in her ear. 'Go to Court Number Two.'

'Er... we have to take you over to Court Number Two now because it's break point. Thank you Gizmo.' The abruptly curtailed interviewee shrugged his shoulders and then found his way, smiling, through the mêlée of officials.

In the corridor, a woman police officer stood looking after the defeated ex-champion in amazement as he strode away. Dismayed, she looked around her and addressed thin air.

'He just knocked it for six.'

Strewn across the parquet flooring of the palatial corridor in the All Countries Tennis Club building were the remains of a huge white urn, a shoulder-high pillar broken into two parts and a scattering of expensive hothouse flowers.

'I'm sure it was just an accident,' murmured the referee as he brushed past her and followed the vandal upstairs to the changing room.

'Mr. Manners! Kindly unlock this door!'

'Go away!'

'Mr. Manners! I am the tournament referee and you will kindly let me in.'

'Go away!'

'Mr. Manners... Kurt... if you don't let me in I shall call security.'

The lock turned and the door swung open. A staring-eyed individual gazed maniacally at the referee.

'Ruined.'

'Come now, Mr. Manners. Surely you can afford to buy us a new one?'

'Not the vase. ME!' He stabbed at his chest. 'I'm skint! This tournament was going to set me back on my feet. That lousy ex-wife of mine took every penny. My accountant's double-crossed me and I can't pay my trainer!' He sank to his knees and sobbed like a baby.

On cue, the trainer appeared in the doorway.

'What do you mean 'you can't pay me', you little oik?'

Kurt Manners had never been called anything but 'Sir' in his entire life and the word 'oik' galvanised him into a steely unfolding of his limbs as he rose to his supreme height of six foot two inches. The sobbing ceased in mid-stream and was replaced by a haughty stare.

'What did you say?'

'Oik!'

'How dare you!'

'Oik!' The trainer took a step forward. 'I've got a wife and three kids and I've run around after you all year, putting up with your filthy temper and the stink of your halitosis and you dare to tell me I won't be paid?'

The thud that connected the trainer's fist to Kurt's jaw had a satisfying timbre that flowed like balm over the referee's raw memories of the spoilt brat of tennis. Kurt reeled back, holding onto his face which bore a look of utter amazement. Surprised by the unexpected assault, he lunged forward, belatedly making a fist and striking out at his assailant who dodged neatly to one side, ensuring that the knuckles of the international racquet-clasping hand smacked into the doorframe with an awesome 'crunch'. Unaware of the damage he had done to his earning capacity, the star waved both arms frantically at the referee with all the gusto of an Italian opera singer.

'You saw what he did. I'm going to sue him for assault. You saw. You saw.' Then 'Aaaah... aaaah' as he looked down at his mangled prize hand and cradled it in the other. The referee smiled deferentially. 'I'm so sorry Mr. Manners. I happened to be looking the other way. Shall I call the doctor for you?'

*

Eight months later the faded and almost bankrupt tennis star found himself sitting in the office of Louisa Luscombe, personality provider to the media. The trim, late middle-aged woman reached down into the deep drawer of her desk, extracted a file and handed it to him.

'What do you think about this?'

On the front it stated, 'The Whizzo Show. Audience-centred entertainment for the ten to fifteens.'

'A kids' show?' queried Kurt nervously.

Louisa spread her hands and placed them gently palms-down on the desk. 'It's peak viewing, Saturday evenings, six 'til seven. Government anti-yob initiative, an attempt to keep the youngsters at home.'

'What's the theme?'

'Ritual humiliation of well-known personalities.'

'What?' exclaimed Kurt, slapping the arm of the settee with his good hand.

'The money's excellent...' cajoled Lou.

'Spill it to me...'

'Five thousand for one show.'

'That's a lot of loot. What do I have to do for that? Public castration?' he asked ruefully.

'No, no. They do sort of party games where members of the audience come up and form teams with well-known people.'

'Yes, and...'

'The winners get great prizes like electronic readers and adventure holidays.'

'And the losers?'

'The celebrity team leader gets a harmless but amusing punishment. Oh... you know the sort of thing... being pelted with cushions or kissing the cameraman. It's a new show. They want you on the first one.'

The fallen star pondered on the state of his bank account, still in the red, and the mortgage company baying at the door.

'I'll do it,' he said flatly.

'That's the man!' exclaimed Louisa. 'Recording is three weeks today. I'll get the contract sorted.'

*

'Are you ready?' shouted Spike the presenter.

The hot, stuffy studio had an atmosphere of hysteria.

'YES!' screamed the audience of youngsters jumping up and down excitedly in their seats. Strobe lighting flickered irritatingly. Thumping music started up. Kurt looked across to see that the other team leader was that schmuck Gizmo Bundi, he who had waltzed off with the tournament trophy last year. He glowered at him. He grinned back.

'Go!'

Well, custard-pie throwing is always a good crowd-pleaser but despite his former prowess at getting his first serves in precisely, Kurt's team lost with only seventy-two strikes to a hundred and fifty. The plastic overalls were inadequate.

'Bad luck, man!' said Gizmo, slapping his adversary on the shoulder.

'Don't do that!' hissed Kurt.

'Wassamatter man? You a sore loser or somethin'?'

'Go for a hike!' snarled Kurt turning to find the presenter sticking a microphone up his nose. Thinking of the five grand, he switched on his best grin and waved at the audience who cheered hungrily, having been primed earlier about the consequences of defeat.

'Hard luck!' said the punk-haired presenter insincerely, slapping Kurt's back a little harder than absolutely necessary. Then he addressed the heaving mass of youngsters baying in anticipation.

'Well, we all know what happens now, don't we guys?'

'Yes! Yes! Yes! Yes!' howled the teenagers at fever pitch, stamping their feet.

'FUNKY DUNKY!' yelled the presenter.

With that, clouds of dry ice fog rolled onto the stage and a large, glass-sided booth descended from the studio ceiling in a shower of glitter and fireworks.

'FUNKY DUNKY!' hollered the hordes.

'Funky Dunky?' queried Kurt, not a little afraid, as he wiped custard pie from the front of his second-best casual suit. Shame about the tie. It had been his All Countries Club one. Spike took him by the elbow, ushered the bewildered stooge into the booth and secured the door with a huge silver padlock.

'Hey! Wait a minute! You can't lock me in...' Panicking, Kurt looked up for a way out, a second before a cascade of multicoloured gunge engulfed him. There was a sensation of being lifted and rotated. Gulping, he swallowed something vile. His eyes were full of the stuff as a he groped to find some way to steady himself. 'Glub! Bloop!' he said as the tank ascended slowly, spun and continued to fill with revolting, thixotropic gloop.

The audience was incandescent with delight but the presenter was the first to realise that the concoction should have stopped flowing by now. Miming to the producer he raised the alarm so that the end credits ran early as paramedics frantically tried to reach the drowning celebrity.

*

'Near-death Experience for Former Tennis Star' was emblazoned on newspaper billboards everywhere. Dozing as he came out of the sedative, Kurt lay back on his hospital bed under a crisp white sheet.

'See you made the front page again, man,' said a familiar voice, holding up the *Daily Review.*

The invalid opened his sore and encrusted eyes. Oh, it was him again.

'What do you want? Leave me alone!'

The stocky, black tennis star swaggered around to the window, hands in the pockets of his stylish slacks.

'You got an attitude problem, man.'

'Stop calling me 'man' for goodness sake!'

Gizmo ignored the order.

81

'You is one hell of an accident-prone guy, if you don't mind my mentionin' it.'

'No need to rub it in. I thought my life was over. What an end to a salubrious career! Drowned in purple blancmange.'

'Hee hee,' chuckled the visitor. He took something from his pocket and lobbed it onto the patient's chest.

'What's this?' Kurt fought with the sheet to get a hand out. His fingers closed on a small round mirror.

'Take a look, dude!' said Gizmo.
Kurt slowly raised it to his face. 'Aaaaa!' he yelped, his expression frozen in horror.

'Wassamatter man? Don't you's like bein' that attractive shade?' sniggered his rival.

'Give me some soap! Send for the nurse!'

'No use fella. They scrubbed you good last night. You's stuck with it for six months! In fact we could say that you's MAROONED!' He guffawed.

'Where's my agent? Give me a telephone!'

'Here, borrow mine.' Gizmo handed over his mobile with a cheeky smile. 'They sacked the bloke that forgot to dilute the dye,' he added 'but that ain't going to be no consolation to you, Plum Tum.'

*

Four days later, Kurt reclined in the barber-style chair of Oakwood Film Studios' medical facial masking department. He had two straws sticking up his nostrils and his face was covered in a thick layer of peppermint green moulding plastic.

'We'll soon be done, Mr.Manners,' demurred the leggy redhead.'

'Ping!' went the timer.

'Now, just relax while I gently peel this away. I'll take the straws out for you.' Kurt snorted. There was a slight ripping sensation as the mould came off leaving his maroon face shiny with lubricant. The girl stifled a giggle. He truly looked like Mr. McCurrant from the blackcurrant juice advert. She cleaned the grease from his face and removed the protective plastic overall.

'Your facial mask will be ready for fitting on Thursday. If you'd just like to pop along the corridor to Room D, they'll see to the other thing for you.'

'Strip off please Mr. Manners!' commanded the buxom, middle-aged woman beautician, 'and kindly lie down on the treatment couch for me. I'll be with you in a moment.'
Sadly removing his clothes before the cheval mirror, Kurt surveyed the formerly light body-hair of his athletic figure. Now maroon all over, he resembled a loganberry. The erstwhile glorious head of blond tresses now looked like something from a cartoon. Even his fingernails were brilliant puce.

Another time, another place, it would have been relaxing and stimulating to be lathered firmly all over and then systematically shaved naked like a baby but the woman handled him like a piece of meat, rearranging his bits to get to the awkward places. His eyes smarted. Somehow he felt emasculated without his body hair. Freshly showered, he looked like a Martian. Only the shock of violet locks gave credence to his humanity. 'Please get yourself dried and put your gown back on and just slip along the corridor to Room J and they'll do the necessary,' said the woman kindly.

Feeling like a shorn sheep Kurt went into the hairdressing section.

'Now, sir,' said Damion, the chief stylist, patting Kurt's shoulders and then waving his hands about expressively. 'We have several options. First there's a wig. No? Doesn't appeal? OK. We can cover your hair with dark brown or black dye but that might look a bit funny when your own comes through again. It would mean a re-tint every fortnight. I don't really know if you can spare the time. OR...' he paused meaningfully, 'we can take the lot off for you!'

Kurt's stomach sank. Bald? Him? Barely holding onto his emotions, he addressed the hair stylist. 'If I have it all shaved off, would it make it easier to wear a blond wig?'

'Oh yes, sir. Indeed, sir. Some of our most FAMOUS clients have gone for that option.' He touched the side of his nose as he silently mouthed a well-known celebrity's catch phrase. 'Then we'll just dye your eyelashes and eyebrows dark brown and Bob's your uncle!'

*

'BBB television is proud to introduce the one and only Mr. Kurt Manners!' the voice-over announced as, sporting a really exquisitely good blond wig and latex face-mask, the indomitable star bounced down the curved staircase to the strains of 'I will survive', thunderous applause and the welcoming hug of Sarky, the septuagenarian host of *Saturday Night with the Splendid Stars.*

The interview went rather well actually. Sarky asked about Kurt's past career and that produced some amusing anecdotes, mainly centred on the changing rooms. Questions about his personal life were parried with adept practice and comments about looking for 'Miss Right'. If nothing else, his former manager, the rat, had taught him how to handle the media. Sarky had the decency not to ask why Kurt was wearing white evening gloves and a cravat like the Brontë sisters' father.

Maybe the face mask felt a little tight. Perhaps the audience wondered if their hero had over-dosed on muscle jabs. Possibly they thought he was a little bit drunk as he conversed through rubbery lips. Nevertheless, the chat finished with enthusiastic applause that was doubled when the second guest star arrived... Gizmo Bundi!

After transmission, graciously declining a glass of something in hospitality and avoiding Gizmo, Kurt, anxious to get home and remove his face mask, made for the car-park which was in the throes of resurfacing and marking out. It was poorly lit but he found his red Fersparti amid the traffic cones and, as he fumbled for his keys, he dropped them and bent down to scrabble on the newly laid tarmac.

'Give us a ride in your nice car Mr. Manners!' said a husky, young female voice.

'Go on, Mr. Manners, please won't you take us for a ride? We'll do ANYTHING you want,' said a second, her curves straining to escape from a low-cut top.

'Absolutely ANYTHING,' opined a third in a micro-skirt.

Terror struck at Kurt's heart. It was one thing to keep the fans at arm's length but quite another to confront them at close quarters.

'It's very kind of you ladies, but I'm rather tired and I want to get home. It is late.'

They clustered around him, their cheap perfume combining with the smell of his latex face.

'Aw go on Kurty darling.' They started to paw at him.

'Let's have a look inside your car.' Micro-skirt bent down and retrieved the keys.

'Oh look! When you press this little button, it opens!'

The sidelights flashed, doors unlocked and the girls piled in.

'I have to go home,' he protested to no avail as they dragged him head and shoulders in after them.

*

'It was a terrible experience,' moaned the shocked celebrity, minus his wig and standing naked except for a rough blanket in the police station medical room. The police surgeon had seen most things in his time but not a bald, maroon, latex-faced ex-tennis player with a yellow stripe painted down the full frontal length of his torso. He felt a mite sorry for the shivering man.

'Here, sir, pull the blanket around yourself better. You're just in shock. Lucky that your friend interrupted. If it wasn't for him goodness knows what else they might have done to you. Try and get some rest.' He closed his case and left as the sergeant looked in.

'I'll just pop up to the canteen and get you a cup of tea. OK? Shall I send your friend in now?'

Kurt nodded silently.

'Hi man. You's one big trouble-finder you is.'

Gizmo stood, leaning against the doorway, cackling with laughter and twirling Kurt's leopard-spot underpants like a windmill. He walked over to the victim, sitting draped in the police blanket, head drooped down, utterly defeated, resoundingly broken.

'You needs somebody to look after you's, man.' He bent over, put his arms around Kurt's shoulders which were now wracked with sobbing, and then planted a kiss on the plum-coloured, shiny head.

'Hey, now, don't take on so. Bein' set upon by women ain't so bad. A lot of us gays has been there.'

Kurt looked up, tears welling over the latex cheeks. 'You knew I was gay?'

'Sure man. We all did.'

Gizmo extended his hand and took Kurt's in a firm grip.

'Welcome to the real All Countries Club, fella.' He grinned and hesitated before saying, 'You know, my friend, no man is an island and there's more than one way to feel marooned.'

Pushing the Boat Out

With a jingle and a clank
In a boatyard on the bank,
The weekend yachts await their captain's hand,
As they clatter, chatter, rattle
In a never-ending battle
With a wind that sweeps like cold knives through the land.

The metal masts all jangle
Lashed by ropes in such a tangle
As the surface of the lake whips up and boils,
While the fluttering of flags
And the soggy sail that sags
Contrive to paint a picture fit for oils.

It's really rather jolly
Now to haul upon the trolley
And to feel your discs impacting one by one
As you strain with pain and heave it,
Sorely tempted just to leave it
And forsake the weekend's masochistic fun.

You look forward through the weeks
To the bilges full of leaks.
Baling out's essential, come what may.
But your wellies keep you dry
'Neath a raining, brooding sky,
When the deck's a-wash with water all the day.

SPORTING HITCHES

There's nothing as exciting
As a Northerly all biting.
At your fingers, ears, and aching teeth it creeps
As insidiously it grips you.
Then maliciously it flips you
In the algae-ridden lake's green, icy deeps.

What drives the Sunday sailor
To take out his mini-whaler,
To do battle with the elements and more,
To tack and turn and glide
Until he ends up on his side
With a rueful glance directed at the shore?

Could it be historic urges
Spawning nautical-like surges
That so drive the weekend matelot to sail?
Is it watery wilds a-calling
Or the wind's seductive squalling
As it whips up to a fearsome, freezing gale?

No, it's not the feel of weather
As it beats you hell for leather
With the waves all crashing, soaking you in spray,
And it's not to share with mates
The excitement of the fates…
The in-laws just arrived for annual stay!

"Your double axel was rubbish!"

"Your triple toe-loop was abysmal!"

"Now's a fine time To tell me you're afraid of heights!"

"Oops!"

"Don't
look
now
but I
think
I can
smell
smoke."

Extract from AIRSHOW ILEX

In the broom cupboard, Roland whispered, 'She's gone but I think we're here in the Press Centre for the night though.' The sound of his face being slapped was followed by a scuffle, a key rattling and the emergence of two perspiring and dishevelled people from incarceration

'Aw Debbie,' he pleaded. 'Give a fella a break. It wasn't my fault.' His paramour was already on her way to the ice-cold water dispenser.

'Don't speak to me,' she hissed, voice laced with anger.

Extract from CARAVAN HITCHES

'I am the ghost of caravanners past,' the apparition said in an echoing, singsong voice. The moonlight shimmered on her silvery white gown as it floated about her in the evening air. Her face was pale, her hair long and white and she had deep, dark circles under her eyes.

Paul stood stock still, the loo cassette handle gripped tightly in his hand. He felt the blood drain from his face and his heart pounded.

Extract from THE LONELY SHADE

Below Par

It's a beautiful day on the golf course.
There's not a sound to be heard
But a zephyr-like breeze
As it teases the trees
And competes with the song of a bird.

Mary B. Lyons is a freelance writer, author, photographer, artist, Illustrator, song-writer and broadcaster whose work has been published in the following:

The Times Educational Supplement
The Lancet
Hampshire the County Magazine
Police Journal
Surrey Monocle
Mail on Sunday (financial pages)
Omega
Machine Knitting Monthly
Hampshire Now
Royal Photographic Society Journal
Pilot
Funeral Director Monthly
Funeral Service Journal
Antique Collectors
SAIFinsight
Business Digest
Local and National papers

Mary has written magazine and newspaper columns and broadcast on BBC local radio and other stations, including hospital radio and Reading 4U. She has appeared on BBC television and also gives talks on a number of subjects to organisations and societies. If you wish to book her for a talk, presentation or photographic exhibition, and require a list of subjects, please write to: Wordpower, P.O. Box 1190, Sandhurst, GU47 7BW, enclosing a stamped, addressed envelope together with an estimate of possible audience size. Bookings are made well in advance.